Ollie Miss

OLLIE MISS

GEORGE WYLIE HENDERSON

WITH AN INTRODUCTION BY BLYDEN JACKSON

The University of Alabama Press

TUSCALOOSA AND LONDON

Introduction copyright © 1988 by
The University of Alabama Press
Tuscaloosa, Alabama 35487
All Rights Reserved
Manufactured in the United States of America

Library of Congress Cataloging-in-Publication Data

Henderson, George Wylie.
  Ollie Miss.

  Reprint. Originally published: New York : F. Stokes,
c1935.
  I. Title.
PS3515.E43422O45   1988   813'.54   87-19242
ISBN 0-8173-0388-X (pbk. : alk. paper)

British Library Cataloguing-in-Publication Data is available.

To
MY SON

INTRODUCTION

Blyden Jackson

Langston Hughes wrote two volumes of autobiography, the first of which, *The Big Sea,* contains an account of the Harlem Renaissance as it appeared to him. He had concluded that the Renaissance expired with, if not before, the spring of 1931, to a significant degree another casualty, he believed, in that second year after the disastrous stock-market crash of the Hooverian Depression. But, of course, no phenomenon of human history such as a period in the arts ever occurs in so conveniently tidy a fashion that it can be dated as if it were a scheduled program extending obediently from one precise point on a calendar to another. There were remnants of neo-classicism (and some neo-classicists) in the nineteenth century. And *Ollie Miss,* published in 1934, is as much a novel of the Harlem Renaissance as Claude McKay's *Home to Harlem,* Jessie Fauset's *There is Confusion,* or Langston Hughes' own *Not Without Laughter.*

The writers, editors, critics, scholars, painters, sculptors, and other personages connected with the arts active as participants in the Harlem Renaissance were neither unaware of their renaissance nor reticent or tentative about what they supposed it to be. They, indeed, were the very ones who ascertained the roots of their renaissance in a difference, radical in nature, between themselves and the black artists, literary and otherwise, of the generation they were superseding. Moreover, it was they, certainly as soon and as clamorously as anyone else, who stipulated this difference. Their immediate predecessors (they regretfully accepted themselves as forced to believe) had been too careful about not offending white America (admittedly because their mere survival, as they saw it, demanded an accommodation from them to whites) either to be truly as free as they might have wished in their assertion of themselves or to take many of the steps, whether in politics or art, that their reason told them were absolutely necessary to bring them closer to a satisfactory position in American affairs. In literature, for example, a set of demeaning stereotypes, largely fashioned, needless to say, by whites, prevailed in the characterization of Negroes and the best that even a black writer of the time as principled as Charles W. Chesnutt was able with any hope of success to do was to try to ameliorate the stereotypes. Not so the writers of the Harlem Renaissance. They expected to have white readers as well as black, that is true. And they certainly knew that no racial millennium had arrived in America in their time. But they did think they had more latitude in which to operate than had had their parents. Moreover, they were young and brash, a new breed. They would cleanse America's literature of the stereotypical Negroes of old, nor would they forget that there was a newness in the Negro of their generation (increasingly emerging from the agrarian South into the urban North), which did seem to reflect, not merely the dispensations of art and the euphoria of Negro ambition, but also genuine advances in Negro achievement. So, they adopted their slogan and their creed, both of which emphasized their break, concerning which they were so insistent, with their immediate past. They were, in their own language, the New Negro. A volume of their literary work and visual art titled exactly that, *The New Negro,* and edited by the Negro Rhodes Scholar, Alain Locke, generally esteemed as more or less the midwife of their movement, was issued in 1925.

The writers of the Harlem Renaissance were the first group of Negro writers to be united by an articulated doctrine and a formulated agenda (aesthetic with political overtones) to which substantially all of the members of their group quite consciously subscribed. These writers were notably a far more cohesive aggregation than any sampling of Negro writers before their time. They were not just bound together as fellow doctrinaires. Except for Anne Spencer and Sterling Brown, who seemed to refrain from the sacred pilgrimage up the Atlantic coast to Harlem most deliberately, all of them met and mingled—at least sufficiently to be considered, in effect, a *salon*—in Harlem. That they did clearly seems to have been no accident. After all, not a single one of them, not even Countee Cullen, long mistakenly thought to have been, was born in Harlem. One of them, Claude McKay, was a native of Jamaica. The rest of them, to recall and review fully the geography of their places of birth and of their wanderings before they converged on Harlem, came from virtually all of America except the Big Sky Country of Idaho, Montana, and Wyoming. Not for nothing did they attach the name of Harlem to their renaissance. For Harlem was clearly a magnet to them, although in no wise the Harlem of the 1960s and thereafter, a synonym (this later Harlem) for drugs and crime and a symbol of despair. Their Harlem was a city of light and almost an end of a rainbow of hope. With much more, decidedly, than merely a metaphorical meaning, it was the capital, not only of Negro America, but of the Negro everywhere. No other locale on God's green earth, in the 1920s, was so well suited to be the habitat of a New Negro as Harlem. The mood of Harlem in the 1920s was that of spring, the season for the new. Not yet then were the migrants to it disillusioned with their vision of it as a promised land to which they were making their way after years of sustaining a concept of it they had refused to lose.

Into this Harlem George Wylie Henderson, the author of *Ollie Miss*, immigrated from Alabama, where he had been born in 1904. He is still one of the more shadowy figures of the Renaissance. No biography of him exists and only the scantiest data about his life seem ever to have been published. It is known that his father was a minister and that he attended Tuskegee, apparently mastering the trade of printing at Booker T. Washington's school. Perhaps he saw Washington, for all of the action of *Ollie Miss* occurs within the vicinity of Tuskegee, almost certainly, it would seem, if only because it was within that vicinity that Henderson spent the most impressionable years of his youth. Certainly, though, he was no stranger to other writers of the Renaissance. To that I can testify as someone who once was privileged to see him and converse with him man to man and eye to eye.

For I went to Harlem in 1931. Actually I went primarily to New York City, and not to Harlem, to attend Columbia University as a graduate student in English. But I lived, for the entire seven months that I spent at Columbia in Harlem at the Y. It was what was later to be called the "Old Y" and was located on the north side of 135th Street between the two famous (to Negroes) avenues, Seventh and Lenox, although only a few feet east of Seventh. A new Harlem YMCA, incidentally, was then under construction, and well along toward completion directly across the street from the Y in which I was a resident and a paying guest. This new Y would be the Men's House of Ralph Ellison's *Invisible Man*. Meanwhile, at my Y I was a neighbor on the fifth floor of Langston Hughes and Zell Ingram, who shared a room and were repatriating themselves from a recent trip together to Haiti and Cuba. Hughes was soon to leave Harlem on a tour of the South to read, as a source of sorely required income for himself and largely to college audiences, from the verse he had already written. But, before he did, I accompanied him and Ingram to dinner with Henderson and Henderson's family at the Henderson *pied-à-terre* in the Dunbar Apartments.

Hughes briefed me a little about Henderson as we walked from the Y to the Hendersons'. He received some aid from Ingram, always more voluble than Hughes. Well before the three of us reached the Hendersons' door I had come to think of Henderson as someone to whom Hughes and Ingram attributed the same kind of identity as they did to themselves. He was to them, clearly I thought I perceived, another artist committed as they were to the cause of the Harlem Renaissance. To my great present regret I made no notes that night. Henderson, I discovered, was working as a printer while he finished a novel—*Ollie Miss*, I must believe, with my present advantage of hindsight. He was married. His wife had prepared our meal. Entertaining us involved, I think I remember, Henderson's suspension of his usual evening occupation, work upon his novel. I do believe the Hendersons had at least one small child. I remember the food we ate at the Hendersons as highly palatable. I remember nothing about it in detail. But I also remember that Hughes, Ingram, Henderson, and I talked long into the night about literature and art (Ingram was primarily a sculptor), but especially about the craft of writing and the definition of responsibilities and opportunities which we felt should govern and inspire, with a due respect for the welfare and future of "the race," black writers and artists in the year 1931. We were having, that is, the same kind of an evening of ideological discussion to which I had been, and would continue to be, a party, eager but virtually silent, at other small, private social occasions where luminaries of the Renaissance and their associates may have gathered during the fall of 1931 and the early months of 1932. I cannot recall whether or not I ever saw Henderson again. I think I did. But the impression that lingers in my mind about him is that of a pleasant host and, since I had read nothing before that night which I could designate as his, of someone whom I conjectured then probably would, given any fair and decent chance, succeed with his writing.

In *Ollie Miss*, Henderson does succeed with the business of composition. The book is spare, both in plot and style. A straight-line narrative about as simple as such narratives can be (and that is very simple), it proceeds directly from the casual, but firm, intrusion out of essentially nowhere of a young black woman, Ollie Miss, into a black folk community of the agrarian South and through a season of planting and harvesting until its final moment, still in that same black community, when the unwed Ollie Miss, recuperating from the almost fatal injuries inflicted upon her by another woman, knows that she will not die of her wounds and begins to anticipate, with anything but fear and loathing, yet rather in a mood somewhat of longing, the birth of the child she is now aware that she is carrying in her womb. Never in *Ollie Miss* is there any doubt as to what *Ollie Miss* is about. It is all about Ollie Miss, most fittingly a titular heroine, whom it obviously pleased Henderson to make a child of nature easily distinguishable from persons possessed, in the eyes of society, of a host of acquired sophistications. She is, this Ollie Miss, uncomplicated. She works and loves, no more. The work she does makes clear her close and instinctual relationship to an earth like that of Hesiod's *Works and Days* and with forms of labor rooted in elemental aspects of human culture. Manually, she tills the ground or tends domestic animals. In love, she loves one man, Jule, and she asks solely of that man that he love her in return. In her character, so transparent, as well as so free of inconsistencies or of anything abstruse, she constitutes a virtually perfect analogue to the aesthetic construct of *Ollie Miss*, wherein no element jars against another and grandiosities and possible intricacies are remarkable only for their total absence.

There are no epic episodes in *Ollie Miss*—nothing such as, for example, the execution of Sidney Carton in *The Tale of Two Cities*, with its imposing historical background of the French Revolution and its action set within the exciting tableau of a passionate mob in one of the world's great cities. The girl, Ollie Miss, of the novel of her name, comes on foot to the dwelling of Uncle Alex, the Negro proprietor of land who answers affirmatively her request to work for him. The world she inhabits of cabins, fields, pools, and paths, or roads often little more than paths, may be traversed on foot. It is a world almost astronomically remote from the crowded, kaleidoscopic world of Chicagos and New Yorks in which she would be anything but at home. Pace within it seems little more than static. It lacks the bustle, the clangor, the congestion, the monumental architecture, and the turbulence of huge centers of population. Its seasons come and go as always, apparently, replicas *in toto* of the rounds of seasons they succeed. In a world as austere as is this one Ollie Miss may be examined with little, or no, distraction from a concentration exclusively on her. She performs well the tasks assigned her by Uncle Alex. She is physically strong, a splendid animal, although she is also decidedly an attractive female. Men, when they see her, understandably desire her, for there is that in the voluptuousness of her body and the liquidity of her movements which inflames the impulse within them to mate. But she is no wanton. She has met this male counterpart of herself whom she deeply fancies and her life revolves around contact with him. Her feeling for Jule, a monomania to some significant degree, still does not prevent her from a constant expression in various commendable ways of her general healthiness of disposition. Her excellence as a hand on Uncle Alex's land derives not only from the strength of her muscles and her athletic skills but also from her philosophic fondness for the respectable discharge of duty. Tragedy invades her life because Jule differs from her in character. Without being terribly dissolute, he can, and does, find himself able to respond to the blandishments of more than one determined temptress, although when a crisis demands of him that he choose between Ollie Miss and another woman, unhesitatingly and decisively he chooses Ollie Miss.

Out of the aftermath to this crisis emerges a conclusive confirmation of the kind of human being Ollie Miss fundamentally is. In adversity her true colors appear distinctly. Without a murmur she prepares herself to face a future with, or without, Jule, but also with a new life on its way of which she must take charge. Uncle Alex has guaranteed her a tenant's cabin and a tenant's opportunities upon his land. Whatever she once projected about Jule, most revealing now are her thoughts about the child she soon will bear. Motherhood will be a new experience for her which she will approach as a welcome test of her ability to shape a beneficent future for some one other than herself. Humble, illiterate, dispossessed, and black, Ollie Miss is as much a proponent of the so-called American dream as any of either its worst or best apostles. She does not disdain upward social mobility for herself. But for the prosperity and happiness of her offspring she seeks that nothing be beyond her reach.

Could there have been a real girl like Ollie Miss, a black girl actually like her, among the black folk of the agrarian South in the America of the 1920s? At one level of discussion there should be no doubt that there could have been. This is the level at which Ollie Miss may be regarded merely as a creature whose magnificent body, as we have already noted, reminds men, whoever they are, of the most sensuous uses of their virility. At such a level Ollie Misses existed in the American South even during slavery. Thomas Stothard of the British Royal Academy painted an aphrodisiac "Sable Venus" in the eighteenth century. Such black women did not disappear with the adoption of the Thirteenth Amendment. But Ollie Miss's novel is, above all, a study of character, with possible references as such not simply to the mental and moral traits of an individual but also to that collective consciousness of the black folk for which the term *soul* may serve as a convenient cognomen. Part of the creed of the Harlem Renaissance, it may well be here remembered, rebuked America, and even black artists, particularly those of the generation immediately preceding the Renaissance, for disparagements of that soul. All of the Negroes in *Ollie Miss* are not so fine as Ollie Miss. Some of these Negroes, indeed, seem far from lovable. But they all incline, like Ollie Miss, not to be stereotypes, and especially not to be monitored prescriptively by models for the formation of themselves conducive to the preservation of American color caste. There is a razor fight (I have never seen, or heard of, a Negro with a razor in a fight) in *Ollie Miss*, the altercation, indeed, in which Ollie Miss is

injured. Nevertheless, it can be argued that *Ollie Miss* belongs—almost surely with premeditation—to the literature of
the Harlem Renaissance and that its protagonist, as well as its
whole gallery of people of her color are products of the mind of
a New Negro, under no circumstances to be confused, however
extreme may be their indigenousness to the Southern soil, their
illiteracy and their other class-related alienations from white
bourgeois America, with racist stereotypes of any kind. A
prime function of theirs is the illustration of black *soul*.

Tuskegee and the renowned school there which Henderson
attended are in Macon County of Alabama. Names of places,
very small towns by no means so large as Tuskegee, such as
Roba, in *Ollie Miss* help to establish the fact that Uncle Alex's
land is in Macon County. It seems conjecturally sound that
Henderson situates *Ollie Miss* where he does because Macon
County, to him, was familiar territory. From one angle of
inspection, then, Ollie Miss is an exercise in American literary
regionalism subject, among other critical approaches, to praise
or blame for the measure of its fidelity to anthropological and
sociological fact. There is here, incidentally, a point that may be
made. By sheer coincidence a classic work in sociology, Charles
S. Johnson's *Shadow of the Plantation*, a study of six-hundred
black families in Macon County, was published, like *Ollie Miss*
(as we have seen), in 1934. It is possible, therefore, to begin, if
not end, an evaluation of *Ollie Miss* for its worth as realism with
a comparison of it to *Shadow of the Plantation*. Johnson sent a
team of scholars into Macon County who were mainly interested in the interpretation of statistics, access to public and
private written records, and the collection of many interviews.
Allowing, however, for the predictable differences in meth-
odology between scientists at work and artists addressing the

Introduction

same subject, *Ollie Miss* and *Shadow of the Plantation* tend to be very harmonious complements of each other. Neither romanticizes the black peasantry of Macon County. Both report an array of human beings who may easily seem less diverse than they are. And while the existence of powerful effects upon the black peasantry of Macon County of economic and political forces far beyond their control (and probably comprehension) and unquestionably inimical to their best interests tends to be argued in *Shadow of the Plantation* in a very open relatively direct manner and with constant resort to easily analyzable documentation as befits the ways of science, innuendo alone, and that of the subtlest kind most apt to stimulate our appetite (and capacity) for reflection upon the nature and significance of things not rapidly to be seen, suggests in *Ollie Miss*, more than other means, the vulnerability of its world to its superior white world. Only two white people do appear in *Ollie Miss*, a sheriff and a doctor, neither of whom, it is true, are caricatured. But their behavior and the deference with which they are received when they descend from their white world into the black world of *Ollie Miss* plainly indicate that one world has been compressed into a separate entity and victimized by the other. No less than *Shadow of the Plantation*, although in terms much more intuitive, does *Ollie Miss* attest to the quasi-feudal subordination, imposed from without, to which the black folk of *Ollie Miss* must adjust their whole lives.

The tone of *Ollie Miss*, however, is neither polemical nor tractarian. A lyricism, rather, genuinely sweet, tempers *Ollie Miss* from its opening pages to its last, making of *Ollie Miss* truly a poem in prose. In perhaps too many particulars *Ollie Miss* fails to possess the dimensions of a masterpiece of the literature of either American or Western culture. It is no *Moby*

Dick, no *Invisible Man*, no *Crime and Punishment*, no *Remembrance of Things Past*. Part of its appeal and its charm, it may well be, is in its slightness. It can be easily read at a sitting, as Poe said a lyric poem should be. But it is not without its very convincing and substantial virtues. Its diction alone deserves high honor and respect. Its syntax matches its diction. Both are exemplary in appropriateness as well as craft. But *Ollie Miss* commends itself, almost surely, to appreciative readers of it, not simply for what it executes deliberately, but at least equally for what, apparently no less deliberately, it refrains from even attempting. It was Keats who once spoke approvingly of "negative capability." *Ollie Miss* abjures much and thereby gains in its measure of accomplishment. On a limited palette it adheres to selected and restricted strategies. Its theme, its fable, its style, all are one in avoiding the massive, the multiple, the obscure, and the complex. What elements are basic in our humanity and our society? Of those the ones most indispensable are represented in *Ollie Miss*, brought to the spire of meaning *Ollie Miss* intends to impart to them in the person and conduct of its fictional protagonist. There is no storm and fury of protest in *Ollie Miss*. There is in it only a tale expeditiously told, so expeditiously that the racism endemic to the world of which *Ollie Miss* clearly is a minted miniature speaks for itself and *Ollie Miss* requires no Zolaesque maneuvers to conflate its art with pleas for social justice. Besides, to write as well as Henderson in *Ollie Miss* is, of itself, to contradict the cardinal premise of racism. The black who should be relegated to the black world of *Ollie Miss* has no business writing an *Ollie Miss*.

Ollie Miss was never a best seller. Only a precious few know of it now. On its merits it belongs in the living traditions of both American, as well as black-American, literature. And no history of the Harlem Renaissance should be without it. *Shuffle Along*, Striver's Row, Sugar Hill, Du Bois' *Crisis* and Charles S. Johnson's *Opportunity*, Marcus Garvey's "Up, you mighty race," Roland Hayes at Carnegie Hall, the "Duke" and Cab Calloway at the Cotton Club and Connie's Inn, Louis Armstrong on stage at the Lafayette, black petty capitalists in Durham, North Carolina, Richmond, Virginia, St. Louis, Missouri, and elsewhere, the first wave of any consequence of black students into the graduate schools of the North and the often lamentably ill-prepared migrants from the impoverished dominions of the vanished Old South flooding the expanding ghettos made by their already transplanted fellows in Northern urban areas like Chicago, Detroit, Cleveland, Philadelphia and New York: all these, too, are part of the history of the Harlem Renaissance, each in its own way. So much of them is gone and irretrievable. *Ollie Miss* remains, a reminder and; somewhat, a resurrection of the time of its creation. But it has other reasons for enduring. *Ars gratia artis* applies to it. Its ultimate warrant for its own preservation inheres in its validity as a work of art. It has a story worth telling that it tells well.

Ollie Miss

CHAPTER I

$\mathbb{D}$USK. . . .

The girl stood in the cabin door. Deep shadows hovered over thickets, over the low, wet bottom along the swamp's edge. The air was cool. Bright patches of purple still showed along the hillsides, and dead pine snags in Alex's new ground reared their chalk-white bodies fiercely against the settling dusk. The swamp was silent and still, like a sleeping child.

The dusk deepened. The girl remained silent where she stood, her eyes sweeping out over the freshly plowed fields to watch the wings of a late crow, low and swift in their homeward flight. Then she turned, picked up a wooden water bucket, and hung it over the back of her head and stepped out into the yard. To-morrow was Saturday, and she was going to Jule's. She hadn't seen Jule for eight weeks!

She went up the trail, across the field, with the

ease and grace of a cat, her arms and legs swinging to a kind of music. She was slim and straight, her skin smooth and dark, like firmly pressed soot. Looking at her face and arms, one was filled with a curious feeling that, to touch them, they would peel off on one's finger like soot, too.

Her shoulders were broad and lean, almost gaunt. Her eyes fixed one simply, the irises a deep white around the pupils. Her lips were free and full and a little sad; but to hear them laugh or sing, one was struck by an innocence that was as primitive and unpretentious as a child's.

The girl entered Alex's yard through the back gate. Alex and Caroline were already in bed, and the fowl on their roost burst into loud, spasmodic cackles at her approach.

The well stood behind the kitchen in the back yard. It was old. Every one on the place came to draw water there. The boxlike enclosure that fitted about the mouth of it had begun to creak and sag, like the joints of an old man. The curbing, once bright beams of new poplar, was black and soggy now. It sprouted green moss and fern plants

2

through its festered sides. Now and again decayed pieces of it broke off and plunged into the depth, carrying with it chunks of dirt and red clay. Once, when it caved in for fair, Alex drew the water off and cleaned the well out. He cut new beams and fitted them into the holes. He fetched white clay and gravel and packed it into the yawning gap about the mouth. Alex was philosophical. Wells and things had to grow old and helpless the same as people.

But such as that had never disturbed this girl. Night after night, she came and let her bucket down into its depth for what it could give. When it couldn't give any longer, she'd seek out another. Or, if she tired of what it had to offer, she'd hit the trail for that which seemed the more appealing. Inside of her, she was simple enough. An impulse seized her and she moved. The mere knowledge of a picnic or a camp meeting, or some "doings" at Roba or the Crossroads, could set her blood pitching to a boiling heat.

But to-night, as she entered Alex's yard, something seemed to throb deep within her. There was the well, the vacant, helpless look of it; and there stood Alex's house. It seemed to squat and clutch at the earth, as though frightened by the sudden approach of night. In it, she knew, Alex and Caroline slept. There was a hall, a pair of steps at each end of it and a room on each side, with a stack chimney at the end of each room, too. A separate pair of steps led into the kitchen that butted the end of one room. Each morning, she sat on those steps and ate her food from a dish in her lap before she went to field.

Caroline would hand her the dish gingerly through the doorway. "Here, chile, take yo' victuals, honey," was all that Caroline would say.

The dish was always full, piled to a level heap. The girl never questioned the source of its fullness. She merely accepted it, braced her knees together, and devoured in silence. . . .

There was the smokehouse, with its dry, salty smell; with hams and middling meat suspended from rafters by tiny rings of hemp; with sorghum and meal and lard in barrels and pot-bellied little kegs. There, too, was the garden; and there, near

4

*With the Coming of the Sun, the Place
Would Throb Anew with the Life of
Cackling Fowl and Squealing Pigs.*

the well, stood the pear tree. This was Alex's, her hitching post,—her nearest approach to home! True, she'd forsake it to frolic at Roba and the Crossroads, to inhale the smell of corn whisky on hot breaths, to dance to a nervous, half-crazed rhythm, strummed hot, like a blue flame, under a burning Alabama moon. But she'd come back, and Alex would let her stay. She could plow. She could hoe and wield an ax.

The girl unwound the rope from a post beside the well, and let it slip through her fingers until the bucket struck the water below. She leaned forward and pulled the bucket up; then lifted it, wet and dripping, to her head.

At the gate, she paused once again to look at the place, at the dim, familiar shapes crouched here and there in the darkness. She listened to the soft rustle of pear leaves, to the gentle cluck of a hen shielding her brood—then moved on.

With the coming of the sun, the place would throb anew with the life of cackling fowl and squealing pigs, with the bray of mare mules and the rattle of trace chains, making ready for the field.

Even now, she could hear Alex's voice: "Bettah start plowin' in th' new ground, Slaughter, you an' Shell, an' git hit swept 'fore hit rain. Willie, you git goin' in th' bottom." And from somewhere a voice would rise and split the dewy silence,—the field cry of a black soul to his ox!

But to-morrow morning, when the sun rose, this girl would be standing on Tan Yard Hill, heading for Jule's cabin, her legs washed a bright black with the morning's dew, her eyes peering, like deadly arrows, into the valley beyond. About her the limy smell of hammock mud and the heavy scent of wet dog fennels would swirl in a fetid eddy. And below the valley would lie still and blue and a little queer in the pure morning's light, and tiny clay chimneys would belch a tiny blue smudge against a pale canopy. . . .

Back in her cabin, the girl placed the bucket on the table and covered it over. The water would keep it tight until she got back.

She lit a torch in the fireplace and gathered her things from nails behind the bed and made a bundle. Shoes, two slips, a dress, and her jumper. She

8

wrapped her lunch in a clean cloth, put it in the bundle, and twisted the whole into a tight knot. Then she fished under the mattress for her razor, slipped it in her bosom, and glanced around the room. She sighed, standing there, her eyes taking in the four walls.

"Lawd, dis is home," she said aloud. "Dis is de only home I got, an' hit ain't enough—"

She broke off and began softly to whistle. She slipped a cap over her head and snuffed the torch. She picked up her bundle and slipped silently into the night. . . .

CHAPTER II

Tего girl (her name was Ollie Miss) had come to Alex's that Spring. At first, it was told that she was from Bot King's place, over the creek. Then Caroline said that she looked like one of those back-water women, what with her broad shoulders and slender hips, and that she must have sprung from Swanson's, below the Stand, or from Black Bottom, up near the Hammock. Later, Nan and Mae Jane had it to tell that she came from the quarters at Roba, and that she had worked her way, by easy stages, from Cotton Valley to Little Texas, and then back up the swamp to the Stand.

Ollie, according to Nan and Mae Jane, begged her victuals at the white folks' kitchens, and worked a day or two in the white folks' fields to get money for cigarette tobacco and an occasional bottle of corn whisky. She slept, so Nan and Mae Jane said, in barns and hay lofts and stacks of sun-baked fodder, and begged rides from accommodating male creatures, who, on Saturdays, went to the 'Boro in ox carts to get the week's rations.

"I speck she eben 'lowed de mens to talk sweet talk to her, too," Nan had said.

"Yeh, I speck she did," Mae Jane had said.

And, finally, in an effort to quell the rumors, Alex had said that the girl was from Duck West's place, down on the swamp—that Duck had raised Ollie. But as to the truth of this, nobody seemed definitely to know, and Ollie herself had never said.

This much, however, was certain: Ollie had appeared at Alex's one evening at dusk. It was May, and the Spring twilight had faded to a symphony of purple and scarlet. The countryside, deep in the lull of its own peace, lay hushed and still; and toward the west, the fast fading afterglow was a somber study in solitude.

Ollie walked up the trail to Alex's house from the big road. Save for a small bundle in one hand, she carried nothing of any tangible importance. Her feet and legs were bare, and her body possessed a mature strength that was plain to see. Her face was calm enough, save for her eyes. Her eyes were

12

vivid spheres of black and white, at once challenging and a little cold.

As she entered the gate, Alex and Caroline were out on the porch, resting through the hour which was a sort of luxury between supper and going to bed. Alex was in his usual chair, with his back tilted against the wall, and Caroline was stretched to her full length on a wooden bench that stood against two upright supports near the porch's edge.

To the right of the steps, cloaked in shadows now, sat Nan and Mae Jane, their arms folded tightly across their breasts. And to the left, toward the smokehouse, sat Knute Kelly and Bell, a bucket of water they were carrying home for the night resting between them. There, too, were Shell and Little Willie and a man named Slaughter.

This Slaughter had come to Alex's a week or two before. He was a powerful figure of a man, standing well over six feet, and he had the habit of strumming a guitar every evening after work, while Shell and Willie harmonized, in subdued tones, to the music that he made.

Slaughter was picking at the strings of his guitar

when Ollie entered the yard. Nan, Mae Jane, Knute and Bell were feasting leisurely over some of the choicer morsels of local gossip, which was their habit. The talk ran something like this:

"You all done heah 'bout Birch, ain't you all?" Nan would say.

"Nuh, Nan, us ain't heard," one of them would say. "Whut's up now?"

"Same ol' thing," Nan would say. "She gwine hab another baby."

"Fer who?"

"Fer dat low-down Cæsar. You all know fer who! . . ."

And so it went, and Alex alone was silent, neither taking part in the conversation of his own accord, nor offering a word of comment even when he was asked.

"Heah dat, Alex?" Caroline would say. "Nope, didn't hear," was all that Alex would say.

So it wasn't strange that Alex was the first to see this girl as she entered the yard.

"Good evenin'," Ollie said. "How you all dis

14

evenin'?" Her voice was soft and low, scarcely above a whisper.

"First straight," Alex said, and stood up. "How be it wid you?"

There was a moment's silence, while the others nodded their heads, or grunted a syllable of greeting. They all nodded their heads. All except Nan. Nan merely turned to one side to spit, then stared pointedly at the girl.

Ollie said quickly, "Oh, I pretty good," and her eyes seemed to soften. She shifted her eyes from Alex's face and let them rest, for a moment, upon first this one and then that one of the group sitting there. Then she turned once again to Alex, and said: "Ain't got a li'l plowin' or hoein' fer a hand, is you? Jes wants to git a ration o' victuals an' a place to sleep fer a night or two."

"Can you plow?" Alex said.

"Kin do anything, mister," the girl said.

"Sweep cotton behind a steer?"

"Sweep cotton behind a heifer, too, ef you gimme one. Had to plow one oncet when us ox tuck an' got sick."

15

Alex chuckled shortly. "Don't plow heifer cows around here," he said dryly. "Keep 'em mostly fer th' milk an' calves they can give. Guess you can milk one all right, can't you?"

"Yeh, I kin milk," the girl said faintly. "Only I is a li'l hongry right now. Ain't et since day befo'e yistiddy."

Nan's mouth, having released its burden of saliva, said nastily: "So dat's whut you is up to, huh, gal? You come heah to eat yo'self a belly full o' victuals, an' den you is gwine on 'bout yo' business, huh?"

"Bettah let me tend to this, Nan," Alex said calmly.

"Yeh, you go on an' tend to hit," Nan said. "You always was a fool to git messed up wid ev'ry stray dog dat comes along."

The girl didn't say anything to that. Her eyes sort of blazed, but her face remained calm enough.

Caroline sat up suddenly straight on the bench, and said: "Daughter, come on up heah on de porch an' take a seat an' rest yo'self, whilst I go fix you some victuals to eat. You knows, daughter, dat us

16

is only got de leavings from whut us hab fer supper, ef you don't minds dat."

"No'm, I don't minds," Ollie said, her voice dropping lower in her throat. "An' I thanks you fer hit, too," she added simply.

Caroline stood up and went back into the kitchen, and the girl came up on the porch and took the seat that Alex offered her. She dropped her hands listlessly in her lap, and her face seemed suddenly to brighten.

Alex sat on the bench where Caroline had been resting. Nan and Mae Jane twisted slightly in their seats to get a more accurate view of this girl, and Knute Kelly and Bell slid down from their seats, said, "Good night, everybody," and disappeared around the house. Only Slaughter, Shell and Willie remained in the same position as they were when Ollie entered the yard.

They were stretched out on the bare floor, in shirt sleeves and overalls, with an elbow propped underneath them for support. Slaughter, the largest of the three, was on the farther side. Shell was in the middle and Willie was on the inside, so that it was quite easy for each of them to see the girl—the entire length of her—as she had stood there in the yard. From the first, they had watched her with a curious fascination; and they continued to watch her now, as she sat there talking to Alex in slow, uncertain tones.

Slaughter's eyes were filled with consuming interest, and Shell and Willie, it was plain to see, were dumbly fascinated by what they saw. The girl—her body—somehow defied the simple garments that she wore. But when Caroline reappeared at the door and told Ollie that her food was ready, it was Slaughter who continued to stare at the doorway through which she had passed, while Shell and Willie relaxed and began to comment and grin in subdued whispers.

To what extent the girl affected Slaughter, he hadn't the slightest notion. He only knew that, within the confines of himself, he felt helpless. His breathing became spasmodic and labored, and a strange warmth filled him. Not even Shell or Willie, both of whom were within the sound of the other's breathing, suspected the extent of Slaughter's

18

feelings. They went on smiling as before. And once Shell turned over and stuck his thumb in Slaughter's ribs, and said: "Whut sey, boy?"

Slaughter turned over on his back and stared up at the ceiling then, his eyes lit with a strange light. And he didn't say anything.

Ollie followed Caroline through the house to the kitchen. There was a bowl of black-eyed peas, with a ham bone lying in them. A pone of cold cornbread was tilted against the edge of the plate, and there stood a glass of buttermilk and a gourd dipper of cool well water.

Ollie sat on a stool at a bare wooden table and ate with a slow, feverish relish. She pulled the pone of bread apart and used each section of it as a temporary spoon. The peas were mellow and sweet, the rich juice tempting with a peppery sting. With each mouthful of peas, she included a morsel of meat, washing the whole of it down with a draft of butter-milk. When the dish was quite empty, she mopped it spotlessly clean; then turned to a saucer of stewed blackberries and dumplings that Caroline had re-

cently placed at her elbow. And this she ate with
the same slow relish, devouring it completely. Then
she drank from the gourd dipper, gulping in the
cool sweetness of the water, until the dipper was
quite empty, too.

Caroline watched the girl intently; and when she
had finished, Caroline said, "Honey, is you sho' dat
yistiddy was de las' time you done eat?"

"Yes'm," Ollie said.

"Well, daughter," Caroline went on, "I ain't mad
or nuthin' lak dat—but tell me, how much kin you
eat when you is eatin' regular?"

Ollie's eyes met the older woman's steadily. She
said, "I ain't sich a big eater or nuthin' lak dat. A
dish o' greens an' a pone o' bread is enough fer me
most anytime. Course I drinks a lot of buttermilk
an' things lak dat, an' evah morning I eats six or
seben biscuits—but dat ain't so powerful much."

"Honey," Caroline said gently, "whut's yo'
name?"

"My name is Ollie," Ollie said, "but most evahbody calls me Ollie Miss."

"Well, Ollie," Caroline went on, "is you sho' you

ain't got a tapeworm or something on de inside of you?"

"No'm," Ollie said, "I ain't got nuthin' lak dat on de inside of me."

"Well, honey"—Caroline found it difficult to be gentle now—"where in de name o' Lord you put so much victuals? Yo' belly don't look lak hits so powerful big!"

"Hit ain't," Ollie said simply, with a little laugh. "I jes laks to clean up whut's on my plate, 'cause I knows de people ain't got nuthin' to throw away."

Ollie laughed again and looked up at Caroline. Caroline smiled a wry sort of smile and looked down at Ollie.

"Well, daughter, I ain't tryin' to rush you or nuthin'," Caroline said, "but soon as you kin find another place to stay, I hopes you'll go on an' stay dere. 'Cause Alex ain't able to feed nobody whut kin eat as much as you."

"But I kin do a lot of work in de field," the girl said defensively. "Evahbody sey dat I is de best hand dey evah had."

"I don't doubt yo' word," Caroline said, scraping

up the dishes. "But Ollie, honey, eben ef you works both night an' day, hit wouldn't be enough to pay fer yo' victuals—"

"Aw, don't take on so, Caroline," Alex said calmly from the doorway. "Let her eat. A li'l victuals ain't goin' to hurt her!"

Alex had come into the kitchen through the bedroom unobserved, and Caroline looked around sharply, somewhat startled at the sudden intrusion of the man's words.

"Hit ain't dat I don't want her to hab de victuals, Alex," Caroline pleaded. "Hit's jes dat I don't want her to make peoples think she ain't got no manners. You know she's a gal, Alex, all by herself, an' hit's so easy fer folks to start thinkin' things."

"Let'm think what they want to," Alex said. "If th' girl is hongry, she's hongry."

Ollie didn't say anything. She simply sat and watched Alex's face, the rich tone of his copper skin, deeply lined and coarsened now, with the flickering flame of the lamplight upon it. And sitting there, Ollie felt drawn to the older man—felt, in some strange way, the presence of his sympathy and,

22

already, his deeply rooted understanding of her. And her heart went out to Alex, beseeching of his friendship, his fatherly protection, and offering the simple devotion of her own loyalty in return.

Alex looked at the girl's face now, and said, "Got enough?"

"Yes, sir, I had plenty," Ollie said, rising to her feet. "An' I thanks you, too, Mistah Alex," she added simply, her eyes clinging to the strange warmth in his friendly countenance.

"That's all right then," Alex said, "ef you got enough." He took a bunch of keys from his pocket, selected one from among the others, and added: "Git yo' bundle an' I show you where you kin sleep."

The girl picked up her cap, and Caroline said, "I git out another quilt, honey, whilst you go fetch yo' bundle. De nights git kind o' chilly long 'bout midnight."

So Ollie went back through the house to the front porch to get her bundle, and Caroline went into the bedroom to get out an extra quilt. Alex re-

mained where he stood by the kitchen door, the
keys ready in his hand.

The porch was deep in shadows now. Night had
come at last, and every one apparently had gone
home to prepare for bed. But as Ollie went through
the hall door, onto the porch, she saw what appeared to be the figure of a man sitting there on
the bench, his elbows propped against his knees.
She paused, and was certain then that it was a man.

She stooped to pick up her bundle, and the figure
came quickly forward to beat her to it. But Ollie's
hand reached the bundle first. Then she straightened, and said, "Thank you jes de same, mistah, but
I guess I is used to pickin' up my own bundles an'
things."

The man drew in his breath sharply, and was
silent. His teeth flashed for an instant in the darkness, then he said apologetically, "Didn't mean no
harm, miss. Jes sort of wanted to give you a hand."
His voice sounded thick and uncertain, friendly
even.

"Didn't figger you meant no harm," the girl told
him, looking directly at his face. "Jes didn't want

24

you to put yo'self to no trouble. I is a 'oman, but I don't guess dat's no reason fer you to do somethin' fer me jes to be doin' hit."

Ollie turned shortly and went back through the house to the kitchen, leaving the man suspended there, as it were, by the tension of his own thoughts. . . .

Seeing Alex standing there with the quilt under his arm, Ollie forgot the incident for the moment, said, "Good night, Mis' Ca'line," and followed Alex out the back door, past the well and out through the back gate, and thence across a hundred yards or so of open field to a tiny one-room shack that stood alone in the open there.

Alex inserted the key in the lock, slipped the chain from the hole, then pushed the door open and lit a match. He went forward to the fireplace at the other end of the room, lit a fat piece of kindling wood, and stood the blazing end upright against the soot-covered bricks.

Ollie followed Alex inside the door and waited there until the torch was lit. Then she dropped her bundle on the bed and proceeded to take in the four

25

walls. There was a window with a shutter on one side facing a solid wall on the other. The fireplace was at the end directly opposite the door through which she had just entered, and the room gave the impression of a huge box, with a gabled roof built over it.

The walls were of poplar logs, ax-hewn and notched at the ends, so that the joints would lap, one over the other, and hold without nails. The rafters for the roof were lean, slender lengths of pine saplings, with the bark skinned free from their slick bodies. So, also, were the joists for the ceiling immediately overhead. But there was no ceiling; only the joists. And during the day or night, one could look through tiny holes between the boards on the roof at dark or light patches of open sky. And when it rained, the water came through the roof and made wet splotches there upon the floor, or dripped into containers that had been placed here and there to catch the water.

The chimney was fashioned with cross sticks and plastered both inside and out with red clay and Johnson grass. The shutter to the window could

26

be opened or shut with a twist of wire that looped over a tenpenny nail, driven into the wall. The bed stood lengthwise along the solid wall, and there was a table in a corner with a wooden water bucket on it, covered over.

On the table beside the water bucket, there were a saucer containing a piece of yellow laundry soap and a tin basin. Above the table, a flour-sack face towel and a tin drinking cup hung from separate nails. On the hearth, before the fireplace, there were pots and skillets, dusty from disuse.

Ollie took all of this in at a glance, while Alex was busy working the key to the door off his ring.

Alex handed her the key now, and said, "We get up about daylight, so the plows kin get goin' by sun-up. Figger to start you in plowin'. But if that don't work out so well, you kin take over a hoe. Got a lot of choppin' to finish befo'e it rains."

"I kin plow all right," Ollie said simply.

"That's all right, then," Alex said, and dropped the bunch of keys in his pocket and moved toward the door.

At the door, he paused and stood there a moment, as though there were something else he wanted to say, but wasn't quite sure that he ought to say it now. So he merely said, "Well, good night," and stepped into the yard.

"Good night," Ollie said, and closed the door, looping the chain through the hole.

She turned and placed another piece of kindling on the fire, then walked over and sat on the side of the bed. She felt tired. Her body felt tired, and her muscles ached.

The torch blazed up again, and she rested her chin on her open palms and looked at the floor. The floor was thick with dust, and she could see the print of her bare toes there. But she felt too tired to do anything about that now.

"Guess I'll git up early enough to do a li'l cleanin' befo'e I goes to field," she said half aloud. "Floor needs scrubbin' an' dat table needs washin' off. Speck dis bed needs scaldin', too. Chinches! . . . Lawd, I sho' don't laks fer nuthin' to be crawlin' ovah me when I is sleepin'!"

She stood up, untied her bundle, and began searching through it for a garment that might be

28

used for a nightgown. But there was none. Everything in the bundle needed washing. So she shook them out piece by piece, and hung them on separate nails behind the bed. Then she spread the quilt over the bed, peeled off the single garment that she wore, and crawled in under the quilt.

She lay quite still, flat on her back, her arms locked in back of her head. She watched the torch blink lower and lower, and her thoughts began to drift. She thought of Alex and Caroline. She thought of Alex as "Uncle" Alex, and she felt now that she was going to like Alex and, in a lesser degree, Caroline, too. Then she thought of the two women who were sitting to the right of the steps, their arms folded tightly across their bosoms, when she entered the yard, particularly the smaller one, with the pinched-up face, called Nan. Then she thought of the incident when she went back to the porch to get her bundle. She wondered about the man, although she didn't know his name. She wondered who he was, and what had been in the back of his mind. What did he want? . . .

The light blinked out. The girl turned wearily

29

on her side, and presently she slept. She had walked from Roba that afternoon, and from the Crossroads during the forenoon. Last night she had been with Jule; and now, to-night, she was alone!

She slept, this girl, soundlessly in the depth of slumber.

CHAPTER III

THE next morning, Ollie was up before daylight. She spread up the bed, washed her face, swept the floor, and poured the water from the water bucket into the wash basin and placed a few of her things in soak to be washed out that evening when she returned from the field. Then she hung the bucket over her arm, pulled the door shut behind her, and stepped out into the open.

Day was breaking now. The grass and surrounding fields were wet and heavy with dew, and the early morning's air was pleasant to feel. Ollie felt rested, her body restored from a night of slumber, and the cool air made her blood tingle with a strange, exotic warmth. She even felt like singing. But she didn't sing. She moved swiftly up the path towards Alex's house, and already she could hear the sound of voices and the cackle of fowl about the yard there. The lot, where the mules and other livestock were stalled, was situated below the house to the rear; and now Ollie could hear the concerted movements of the animals, pawing their hoofs, biting corn from the cob and crushing it with their teeth.

A mule brayed; a pig squealed; and another day on the farm had begun. Man and beast felt fresh and rested, ready for another day in the field. But only the sweat and aches of their tired bodies would see it close.

Caroline was in the kitchen getting breakfast. Alex had had his coffee and was down at the lot among the livestock now. As Ollie entered the kitchen, Caroline was placing two fried eggs gingerly upon a plate.

"Mornin', Mis' Ca'line," Ollie said.

"Mornin', Ollie," Caroline said, turning swiftly. "How you dis mornin'?" Caroline picked up another skillet and placed a half dozen slices of salt bacon on the same plate.

"Oh, I pretty good," Ollie said in a low, musical tone, her eyes fresh and sparkling.

"Dat's good. You sleep well?" Caroline felt friendly and talkative this morning.

"Yes'm," Ollie said. "I always sleep well."

"Well, heah is yo' breakfast," Caroline said sooth-ingly. Then she added, "You know, honey, Alex gits mad when he don't gits de plows goin' by sun-up. So you bettah eat yo' victuals an' git through 'fore Alex gits back from down to the lot yonder."

"Yes'm."

Ollie sat down to the table, and Caroline brought butter and molasses and a plate filled with hot bis-cuits, and explained: "Us don't eats buscuits on week-day mornin's, daughter, 'cause flour is too high. De buscuits us saves fer Sunday victuals. But I fix dese fer you 'cause dis is yo' furst mornin'. . . . Alex don't eats nuthin' but coffee fer his break-fast, an' I don't eben eats dat. So you see, honey, dat us ain't a eatin' crowd."

Ollie said, "Yes'm" again, and proceeded with her meal. Besides biscuits, eggs and bacon, butter and molasses, there was a glass of clabber at her elbow. Ollie had told Caroline that she didn't drink coffee, and Caroline had said that all the buttermilk was gone.

"You drunk de last drap last night," Caroline reminded her plaintively.

"Dat's all right ef you ain't got none," Ollie said. "But sweet milk makes me sick to de stomach."

So Caroline skimmed the cream back and poured Ollie a glass of clabber from a stone jar that was ready to be churned.

Nan and Mae Jane came up the steps into the kitchen, with a pail of fresh milk in each hand. When Nan's foot touched the bottom step, she saw Ollie sitting at the table, and something within her seemed to stiffen. Nan said loudly, "Mornin', gal! Can't you stop eatin' long enough to sey good mornin' when you hears peoples comin'? Whur is yo' manners at, anyhow?"

Ollie winced, said through a mouthful of food, "Mornin' to both of you all," and looked around. "Didn't see you all tell jes now," she went on, "an' den my mouth was too full to sey anything."

Mae Jane nodded, and said, "Mornin', daughter." But Nan said sourly, "Dat ain't no excuse, gal. Oughtn't to stuff victuals in yo' mouth lak you ain't

34

nebber had a mouthful in yo' life, nohow. 'Side o' dat, I don't wants yo' good mornin' now, 'cause I tuck an' had to ast you fer hit—"

"Now, Nan!" Caroline pleaded.

"Now nuthin'!" Nan said. "Dat gal ought to hab some manners."

Ollie didn't say anything. Just went on with her breakfast, while Nan poured the milk through a strainer into the churn.

When Nan was gone, Caroline said, "Don't pay Nan no mind, honey, 'cause Nan is jes funny lak dat."

Ollie took a sip from the glass of milk at her elbow, and still she didn't say anything.

Alex came through the back gate into the yard singing, and Caroline said, "Dat's Alex now—"

Alex always sang hymns in the morning when there was important work to be done in the field. He lined out two lines of each verse at a time, then raised the tune in common meter:

> "*A charge to keep, I have,*
> *A God to glorify . . .*"

35

When Alex entered the kitchen door, Ollie had finished eating and was standing there beside the table, her cap ready in her hand.

"You all ready, is you?" Alex said, smiling.

"Yeh, I is ready," Ollie said, and her eyes softened. "How you dis mornin', Uncle Alex?"

"First straight, thank you," Alex said. "How's Ollie?"

"Pretty good"—softly.

Alex chuckled. "Come pretty near fo'gettin' my manners."

"Oh, dat's all right, Uncle Alex," Ollie said, and Alex chuckled again.

He went on into the kitchen, took a spoonful of lard from Caroline's lard can, and Caroline said: "Alex, why in de name o' Lawd don't you buy axle grease an' quit usin' up my lard on dem ol' plows an' things!"

"Come on, Ollie," Alex said, ducking swiftly out of the kitchen, "so we kin get the plows started before th' ol' hen gits mad. Th' ol' hen gits mad when you take her lard, Ollie."

36

Alex chuckled again, and Caroline got angrier still, in a pleased sort of way.

Ollie followed Alex out through the back gate. It was broad daylight now, and toward the east, the sky was a freshly tinted rose where the sun would soon rise. Nearer, in the distance, field larks rose and winged their way through the cool, crisp air. And nearer still, the caw of crows, feeding in the lowlands to the right of the lot, could be heard.

But Ollie wasn't concerned with the matter of these things now. Her eyes watched intently the three men she saw placing the mules in harness down there by the cribs. The largest of the three, she knew, was the same person who was sitting on the porch when she returned to get her bundle last night. The other two, she had reasons to believe, were the ones who were with this man when she entered the yard. And seeing them now, she knew they were hired hands, working for Alex.

Seeing Alex and the approaching figure of the girl, the three men looked at each other and grinned, and Ollie could see that their lips moved in low speech. She couldn't hear what they were saying, and the matter of this didn't seem to concern her now. She merely watched them at their task and, drawing closer, she saw that they watched her from the corners of their eyes.

Alex introduced the men to the girl, pointing to each, in turn, saying: "That's Slaughter; this is Shell; an' that's Li'l Willie over there." Then he added, "Boys, this is Ollie—Ollie Miss. She's goin' to work right along with you all."

The men grinned and nodded their heads, and Ollie said, "Pleased to meet you all."

The largest, of course, was Slaughter. The tall, thin one, with the long feet and gangling arms, was Little Willie. Shell was the shortest of the three, and the whites of his eyes were kind of red-looking.

Alex said now, "Ollie, you kin plow the gray mule." Then he turned to Little Willie and said, "Willie, you bettah take ol' Tom," and the other two men—Slaughter and Shell—laughed. Old Tom was the steer.

Willie said whiningly, "Un' Alex, dat cow is too slow. De sun'll blister me whilst he's tryin' to make

38

up his mind to git to de other end of de row. Ought to give him to Shell—"

"Whut you wanna give him to me fer?" Shell said. "I don't want him!"

"Gawn, Willie," Alex said, "and plow the cow! You know you is lazy, anyhow."

So Willie plowed Tom and Ollie plowed Gray Ida. Shell plowed the little mule, called Queen, and Slaughter went forth behind the other, Ida, commonly known as Red Ida.

Alex started the plows that morning in the peach-tree cut, across the branch from the new ground. He set the sweep for Ollie, watched her plow a round or two, then proceeded on his way across the branch to the new ground, where the hoe hands had already begun to gather for the day's work. Alex wanted to finish chopping that day before it rained. Mity and her crowd were coming over to help out. Nancy Franklin's crew, Ed and Jack and Johnny, would be there. And from Alex's own place, there would be Nan and Mae Jane, Knute Kelly and Bell, and Pink and her crowd.

Caroline would remain at the house to do the

cooking. Alex paid the hoe hands fifty cents a day and one meal of victuals.

The plow hands settled down to the day's grind, as Alex went slowly across the field to the new ground. The first round or two were a bit awkward for Ollie. It was the first time she had done any sweeping that year. The cotton stalks were small, the rows freshly chopped, making the first sweeping far more difficult than later plowings.

But after the first round or two, Ollie began to warm to her task. The set of the plow in her hand became easier, and she found little difficulty in brushing the right wing of her sweep against the tender stalks, without plowing into their roots. There was little or no talk at all between the hands, save for a word spoken now and then to the mules. Once Little Willie went into a lengthy dispute with old Tom, finding it necessary to do a neat piece of cursing in the bargain, only to loose the major part of the encounter to old Tom in the end.

The cow, it seemed, had certain fixed notions as to where he should walk in the middle between the rows, while Willie had notions of his own. Old

Tom pursued a course in the center of the broad middle. The cow, apparently, liked his freedom. So Willie began to tug at the plow line and the cow grew fretful and broke into a gallop, plowing up ten or twelve feet of perfectly good cotton before Willie could restrain his efforts.

Slaughter and Shell laughed heartily and offered a few jokes at Willie's expense. But Ollie didn't laugh, and if the incident struck her as being humorous or otherwise, she gave no indication of it. She simply went on with her plowing, as though the incident had never happened.

Aside from this, things moved along smoothly enough, and still there was little or no talk even among the men. Whoops and field cries came from the new ground now, as the hoe hands got under way, and snatches of corn songs drifted across open acres from neighboring fields.

Ollie plowed row for row with Slaughter and Shell, lifting her plow at the ends and turning her mule into the next row a foot or two ahead of theirs. As a matter of fact, Slaughter and Shell found it increasingly difficult to keep the pace that

41

was being set by this girl as the morning wore on. They kept watching Ollie, watching the strides of her mule, and now and again they urged their own animals along to keep abreast. But, finally, Shell gave up the struggle, and Slaughter and Ollie stepped on out in front, side by side, their plows singing beneath the sandy loam.

But, even now, Ollie made no effort to break the silence that had engulfed them, and Slaughter didn't speak at all. He simply watched the girl, his eyes glancing toward her and away, as though she possessed for him a growing and vital fascination. His lips were pressed tightly together and his hands gripped the plow handles with a firm hold. Once his eyes glanced up and met hers, and his own dropped again. Something within him seemed to quicken. It was as if some part of her had touched a secret depth within him, opened it up and laid it bare, exposing it to the sensitive elements of her own being. To him, the girl might have been a drug—a kind of obsession, cruel and consuming. The incident of the past evening was still fresh in his memory.

42

Slaughter plowed on. The sun was getting hotter, and he seemed helpless and confused. Once he caught his breath sharply and held it. And once he said, "Git up, Ida—damn you! Git up! . . ." And, then, there was silence.

Ollie, on the other hand, watched her plow and seemed scarcely conscious of the man at all. She gave her attention wholly to the task at hand, watching her mule, and listening to the song of her sweep beneath the soil. Neither the heat of the sun, nor the force of it against her back, appeared to disturb her. She plowed serenely on, as though it were just another day.

Finally, as they approached an end, near a thicket, Slaughter said, "Speck we bettah take out an' water de mules. 'Bout time I guess." His words were toneless.

"All right," Ollie said, and she didn't lift her eyes.

She stopped her mule and set her plow. Then she released the hame string, drew the harness from the animal's back and followed Slaughter into the thicket, while Shell and Little Willie were turning their plows at the other end.

Entering the thicket, Slaughter said suddenly, "You ain't still mad 'bout las' night, is you, miss?" His breathing became suddenly pronounced.

"Nuh," Ollie said, "I ain't mad. Ain't nuthin' to be mad about."

The man looked relieved, his lips twisting themselves into a slow grin. He said, "Jes thought you mought be mad 'cause I—I tuck an'—"

"Nuh," Ollie told him, in the same indifferent tone, "no need to git mad 'cause you spoke to me or nuthin' lak dat. Jes didn't want you to think you had to do somethin' fer me jes 'cause you is a man an' I is a 'oman, dat was all."

Slaughter was silent. Then he said again, "I jes thought you mought be mad, dat was all."

They came to a small brook now, deep in the recesses of a lush thicket. The air here was light and cool, and the leaves on the trees made dappled shadows on the bright, sunlit water. The water was swift in its movements, but shallow, and a hole had been dug beneath a clump of alders to permit a greater depth for drinking.

Ollie led her mule in first, while Slaughter waited

44

with his upon the bank bordering the stream. Then he allowed Red Ida to go down of her own accord, and he turned to Ollie and said, "Wouldn't mind ef I dropped by to see you sometimes an' mebbe walk wid you to church, would you?"

"Wouldn't make much difference to me," Ollie said. "I ain't sich a hand fer comp'ny lak dat, an' I mostly goes to church by myself when I goes."

"You means, you don't laks mens fer comp'ny?"

"Oh, I laks mens fer as dat goes," Ollie told him.

"Den—den you means, you don't laks me?" Slaughter felt the sweat break out on his forehead, but his eyes didn't leave the girl's face.

Ollie twisted her body around to face him squarely. His eyes, she saw, were those of an eager child's, deeply set and strangely alive. She looked at his eyes. She looked at his face, too. His face, the jet flesh of it, was drawn and wet-looking. Ollie said slowly, "Whut difference would it make ef I laks you, or ef I don't?" And her own eyes, luminous and a bit curious now, didn't swerve by so much as an inch from his face. They held it—

45

watched it—as though they sought a deeper significance in his countenance there.

Slaughter didn't answer. He released his gaze and looked away. He looked hurt. His eyes looked hurt and his shoulders seemed suddenly to sag. He put out his hand and caught hold of the mule's rein as she backed up out of the stream, the water dripping from the bit in her mouth onto his hand. And, still, he didn't say anything. And saying nothing, he seemed to answer her question with an eloquence that wouldn't have been possible had he used his lips.

His silence said that it would make a difference to him. But if the girl saw the answer, she gave no sign of it. She simply looked at Slaughter, at the back of his neck and the droop of his shoulders, with a cold sort of curiosity in the vivid black dots of her eyes.

Shell and Little Willie came into the thicket now. Shell was leading Queen and Willie was swinging back on the plow line behind old Tom. Old Tom was all hot and bothered, and he was panting at a furious rate. Nearing the branch, the cow made a

46

dash for the water, snatching Willie off his feet and dragging him the remaining few feet to the pool's edge.

Willie cursed shortly, eloquently. And Slaughter said, "Sey, boy, don't you know dere is ladies present?"

"Yeh," Shell said, glancing at Ollie, "watch dat big mouth o' your'n."

"Excuse me, miss," Willie said, picking himself up off the ground. "I didn't means no harm. Dat durn cow tuck an' made me sey dat."

"Oh, dat's all right," Ollie said, looking at Willie. "'Tain't no need to 'pologize. A li'l cussin' ain't nuthin' nohow, an' cussin' in front of 'omans is de same to me as cussin' in front of mens. Cussin' is jes cussin'—dat's all."

Shell had stood there with his mouth open, watching Ollie, as she and Slaughter led their mules out of the thicket. Willie was still crouching there on the ground, digging his thumbs into the damp earth.

When Ollie and Slaughter were out of earshot, Shell turned to Willie and said: "You hear dat, boy?"

47

"Hear whut?" Willie said.

"Dat whut she sey 'bout cussin' in front of 'omans is de same as cussin' in front of mens?"

"Yeh, I heard," Willie said. "Whut about hit?"

There was a pause. Then Shell said, "Well, whut kind of 'oman is dat?"

"Whut you mean—'whut kind of 'oman is dat'?" Willie said. "How you know dat she's a—" Willie checked himself and his eyes sparkled maliciously, his lips grinning.

Shell continued to watch after Ollie and Slaughter until the intervening thicket completely blocked his view. Then he turned to Willie, and said: "Whut wuz dat you sey, boy?"

But Willie only said, "I nevah said nuthin'," and looked up innocently at Shell's face, the whites of his eyes gleaming.

Shell called Willie a dirty liar on his own account, then led Queen down to the water's edge to drink. . . .

Ollie and Slaughter returned to their plows and continued until noon, side by side, without further

48

*Ollie and Slaughter Returned to Their
Plows and Continued Until Noon.*

comment. Once, Slaughter asked Ollie whether her sweep was plowing smoothly, and Ollie had said that it was.

"I kin take up de traces fer you, ef hit's plowin' too deep," Slaughter said.

"Nuh," Ollie told him, "hit's all right lak hit is. Thank you jes de same."

So they had continued, and for the first time that morning Slaughter seemed absorbed with his own thoughts. But Ollie watched Slaughter, the side of his face, the set of his shoulders, and the grip of his hands on the plow handles, where the plow lines looped over his wrists. Actually, for the first time, the girl seemed curious about the man. Even conscious of him. But she said nothing and the plowing proceeded. It was around eleven o'clock then.

Alex came back across the field and paused for a moment. His mission now was simply to see how the plows were progressing. The hoeing was well under way, with Knute Kelly carrying the lead row.

Alex said to Ollie, "Well, how goes it?"

"Pretty good, Uncle Alex," Ollie said, with a little smile.

"Like plowin' wid the boys?"

"Hit's all de same to me, Uncle Alex," Ollie said. She stopped her mule and mopped her face. The sun was getting hotter. Sweat trickled down her face and her clothes had begun to stick.

"They is treatin' you all right, ain't they?" Alex said, and glanced at Slaughter. Slaughter was turning his mule into the next row to start the furrow back to the other end. He didn't stop. Neither did he turn his head. He spoke once, gently, but his words were addressed to his mule.

"Sho, dey is treatin' me all right, Uncle Alex," Ollie said, and smiled again. Then she added: "Guess you won't hab to worry much 'bout nuthin' lak dat, Uncle Alex."

Alex stood there a moment longer, watching the girl, as she swung her plow into the next furrow. Then he moved on across the field towards the house.

CHAPTER IV

At noon, Caroline beat on an old sweep with a hammer and the plowing ceased. Ollie unhitched Gray Ida and jumped sideways onto her back. Slaughter and Shell rode straddle, and Little Willie plodded homeward in the dust behind old Tom.

The mules were stalled and fed. Ollie shucked her share of the corn and placed it in a separate pile there in the trough. Slaughter and Shell had offered to take care of the feeding for all the mules. But Ollie had said, "Nuh, I laks to do my part de same as anybody else."

So the three of them had tended the feeding for the mules, while Little Willie watered old Tom, tied him to a corner of the crib in the shade, and ripped apart several bundles of fodder for his feed. Then they proceeded to the house, the three men walking shoulder to shoulder a few paces to the rear of Ollie. None of the men spoke. They simply walked be-

53

hind this girl and watched her slow, graceful movements as she went up the path to the house.

Caroline had set the table for the hands on a
makeshift scaffold there in the yard. There was a
bench, together with boxes and chairs, upon which
the hands could sit while they ate their meals.
There were soap and water and a wash basin on a
crosspiece outside the kitchen door. And there was
a towel suspended from a nail for common use. It
was to these that Ollie went to wash her face when
she entered the yard, and the three men took turns
washing their faces after she had finished.

The hoe hands began to arrive from the field now,
with empty water jugs under their arms, the dust
sticking to the sweat on their faces, to their eye-
brows, and to the smooth, bare surface of their arms
and legs, too. They came together in a huddle there
by the crosspiece, laughing and talking and washing their faces, while Caroline carried steaming
dishes from the kitchen out to the scaffold. Voice
after voice called out: "Howdy do, Mis' Ca'line?"
Or, "How you is dis day, Aunt Ca'line? . . . I ain't
seen you since de last time!"

And Caroline would pause, a steaming dish of greens or peas balanced in her hand, and say smilingly: "Who is dat speakin' to me?"

"Hit's me," a female voice would say.

"Me who?" Caroline would insist.

"Mity."

"Lawd, Mity, honey!" Caroline would say. "Gal, I lak to not of knowed you! How you do, anyhow?"

"Oh, I all right, Mis' Ca'line," Mity would say, and everybody would laugh. They all knew Caroline recognized Mity's voice at first. Caroline knew the sound of every one's voice. That was just Caroline's way, and they liked it, too. It gave each of them a chance to have "Mis' Ca'line" make a fuss over them.

Alex came through the hallway and out into the back yard now. Alex had been up the big road to look at the crops in that section. Streams of sweat were trickling down the sides of his face, and huge spots of sweat showed through his shirt front and along his shoulders, where the suspenders were strapped against his back. But he said cheerfully,

55

"Guess you all is ready to eat me up now, ain't you?"

"Sho, Uncle Alex—sho us is!" they chorused loudly, laughing. "An' when us git through eatin' on you, dere ain't gwine be nuthin' to you left needa, Uncle Alex. Nuthin' but de bones!"

Alex chuckled good-naturedly at this and the group of them laughed heartily, Mity's largest boy, Luke, letting out a loud swamp whoop.

The hands took seats about the scaffold now. Ollie sat on a box at one end, and Slaughter sat on a bench to the right with Shell and Little Willie. Caroline brought out several plates filled with corn-bread, two pails of buttermilk, and the meal proceeded. Ollie hadn't said anything during the preliminaries preceding the meal, and now she ate her food in silence, speaking only when some one spoke directly to her. Slaughter was silent, too. But Shell and Willie kept pace with the others, eating and drinking, laughing and joking.

It was Mity who turned to Slaughter and said, "Hey, Slaughter, whut's eatin' on you? You ain't said a word yit."

"Yeh," Luke said, "he settin' der wid a long face

lak he gittin' ready to drap dead." And there was
laughter.

But Slaughter made no reply, and Mity turned
now to see a strange face at the other end of the
table. The face was that of a woman, and the
woman was Ollie Miss. For an instant, Mity sat
there looking at Ollie, her mouth opened wide,
showing a mouthful of well-ground food.

"Dat's de new gal Uncle Alex done hired, ain't
hit, you all?" Mity said.

"Yeh, she de one," somebody said. And Mity got
up and walked to the other end and stood there beside Ollie's seat.

"Honey," Mity said to Ollie, "whut's yo' name?"

"Ollie," Ollie said, without lifting her eyes from
her plate.

"An' you is de new gal Uncle Alex done hired?"

Ollie said, "Yes'm," and carried another helping
to her mouth.

"Well, daughter," Mity said now, "you is a right
pretty-lookin' gal, does you knows dat?"

"Yes'm, I knows hit," Ollie said evenly. "But dat
don't make no difference."

57

"Nuh, hit don't—not to me, hit don't!" Mity said. "But hit do makes difference to de mens, honey!" And, once again, there was laughter.

But when Ollie said, "All de same, I ain't got nuthin' no other 'oman ain't got," the laughter ceased, except for an off-cue snicker by Luke. And Mity returned to her place at the other end of the table.

"Honey," Mity said now, "dat wa'n't sich a nice remark you makes den."

"No'm," Ollie said, "I guess hit wa'n't." And she continued with her meal.

After dinner, the older women lit pipes and the younger ones took dips of snuff. The men bit off large chews from plugs of Brown Mule, and Ollie pulled a sack of tobacco from her bosom and rolled a cigarette.

The others watched Ollie intently. But they didn't say anything. They simply watched out of round, innocent eyes, while the girl rolled the cigarette expertly between her fingers and sealed it with a lick of her tongue, as if they wanted to say, "Jesus, you know dat's a sin! . . ."

58

Nan and Mae Jane entered the yard then, puffing heavily, their faces ashy with dust. Nan and Mae Jane were always the last to come from the field. Usually, they went visiting to see what they could hear—to get the latest news. And, to-day, they had walked two miles out of the way to visit Sis' Ida.

When Nan entered the yard, Mity said, "Whur you all been, Nan?"

"None of yo' business," Nan said shortly. "Been tendin' our business an' leavin' your'n alone, ef you got to know!"

Nan turned then and spotted Ollie with the cigarette in her mouth. Nan's lower lip dropped. Her eyes narrowed, and the tiny, black pupils seemed to glint sparks of pure fire. Nan walked over to Ollie, took her pipe from her teeth, and said, "Gal, whut's dat thing you got 'twixt yo' lips?"

" 'Tain't nuthin' but a cig'ret," Ollie said. "Can't you see hit, Mis' Nan?"

"I got a good mind to slap hit down yo' throat, too," Nan said. "You brazen heifer, you!"

"I wouldn't do nuthin' lak dat, ef I was you, Mis' Nan," Ollie said simply, and there was a pause.

59

Nan stood there in conscious, tight-lipped silence, and the others gathered around, wide-eyed and expectant. Their faces were drawn, their mouths shut, and there wasn't a sound. Apparently, no one breathed but Nan, and now her breathing rose to a sharp, hissing sound, as she sucked the air into her lungs through her teeth.

Alex and Caroline stopped their meals and came to the kitchen door. Caroline was visibly nervous.

Alex said calmly, "Whut's th' matter, Nan?"

"Whut's de matter?" Nan said, turning to face Alex. Then she pointed her finger at Ollie, and said, "Don't you see dis young heifer standin' heah wid dis cig'ret thing burnin' 'twix' her lips?"

Alex chuckled and said, "Now, Nan, gawn an' eat your victuals an' quit frettin'! Ollie ain't hurtin' nobody. Anyway, ain't you smokin' a pipe?"

"I don't care ef I is," Nan returned hotly, "ain't no young gal gwine stand in my presence an'—"

"Gawn, Nan, an' eat yo' victuals," Alex repeated. "Don't aim to tell you that any more."

A silence fell then, and Mae Jane took Nan by the arm and led her away.

Caroline said wistfully, "Ollie, honey, throw yo' cig'ret away so Nan kin shut her mouth an' us kin hab a li'l peace. Us jes wants a li'l peace, daughter, ef you don't grudge us dat."

So Ollie took a final puff on her cigarette and tossed the butt far out into the yard, and everybody seemed relieved except Nan. Nan twisted free of Mae Jane's grasp and stood there glaring at Ollie, her eyes hot with rage, her bosom heaving.

Ollie turned and sat down on the crosspiece there, her shapely bare legs swinging rhythmically. Alex and Caroline returned to their meals, and the group there in the yard broke up in pairs and threes, and the talking and the joking went forward as before. Only Ollie remained silent and alone.

At two o'clock, the hands returned to the field. The hoe hands finished the new ground by the middle of the afternoon, and Alex brought them across the slue and started them in the ten-acre cut across the road by the persimmon tree. The plows continued in the twenty-acre stretch on the right hand side of the road where they had started that morning. By nightfall, if things went well, they would still have a good half day's plowing before them there the following day. Then Alex would start them in the new ground and get that swept by noon of the third day, the weather permitting.

The work with the plows went forward pretty much the same as it had that morning, except that Willie was constantly in trouble with old Tom. The sun, throughout the long afternoon, was extremely hot and the cow was fretful. Once, it took the combined efforts of the three men to restrain the waywardness of the steer, and even Ollie had to lend a hand in the end.

It wasn't so much the position that Tom took in the middle between the rows now. It was simply that he had no inclination to plow at all. Old Tom balked, foamed at the mouth and kicked at the traces, and once or twice he succeeded in getting his hind legs completely out of the harness altogether. Then the trace chains had to be unhitched and rehitched again, in order to get the steer's rear end back into a normal, working position for plowing. Once, too, Shell had to lead the cow for a spell, give

62

him a practical demonstration of the thing that he was supposed to do.

Aside from this, the plowing progressed at a healthy rate, Ollie setting the pace all the way. And, still, there was little talk. Ollie simply watched Slaughter, and Slaughter watched his plowing with the same silent intensity that had characterized his attitude during the latter half of the forenoon. Neither Shell nor Little Willie had said anything to Ollie, and she seemed scarcely conscious of them at all. She simply watched Slaughter. Whether she was just curious, or more deeply disturbed by something she saw within the man, one couldn't tell. She went on with her plowing and Slaughter appeared to sink deeper and deeper into the silence that had engulfed him. Even when they took their mules to water during the middle of the afternoon, he said nothing beyond the civil reminder, " 'Bout time to water de mules, I guess." Actually, he seemed glum, deeply hurt.

The afternoon wore on and, once, Ollie burst forth into song. Her voice was rich and low. Then she began to whistle—whistle with the skill and feeling of a man. Whistling seemed to do something to her, for her face lit up, as though her thoughts and feelings weren't confined to the plow beneath the grip of her fingers, nor to the men who toiled by her side. It was as if she were thinking of Jule and the weeks that had just passed. The cruel sweetness of hot nights, and the crueler sweetness of burning passion, too. The heat of night was transitory, an inanimate thing. She could escape that. She could even endure it. But the still, fierce warmth of flaming passion! That was a part of her—a part of her youth, her being. A part of her body. It was her body, the thing that gave her flesh, her youth, its significance. Could she escape that? . . .

At sundown, the plowing and hoeing ceased and man and beast plodded homeward to a night of slumber. The mules were tired and their bodies smelled of sweat. The hands were tired and their bodies smelled of sweat, too.

Ollie led Gray Ida by the reins, the trace chains jingling in the dusk. The three men followed with their animals, one after the other, single file. Alex permitted the hands to ride the mules at noon. But at night they were too tired, and so they had to be led.

After the feeding, Slaughter broke his silence for the first time. He turned to Ollie, and said, "Dere's going to be a li'l party up to Lucy West's house to-night, ef you care to go 'long. Nuthin' rowdy. Jes a li'l clean fun wid music, an' mebbe a li'l dancin'."

"Some other time, mebbe," Ollie said. "But I guess I won't go to-night. I feels a li'l tired an' I has a li'l work to do 'fore I goes to bed."

"Won't last long," Slaughter urged. "'Bout a hour or two, mebbe, an' de music is kind o' nice to listen to. Jes thought—"

"Yeh," Shell said, "they has good music, all right, 'cause Slaughter is one of de main ones."

"I believe you all, all right," Ollie said. "But I guess I won't go dis time."

"All right, den," Slaughter said, and Ollie walked on up to the house without further comment.

Ollie ate her supper alone in the kitchen. Caroline and Alex had eaten theirs. Then she filled her bucket at the well, balanced it on her head, bid Caroline and Alex good night, and proceeded to her own shack.

She rubbed out the things she had put in soak that morning and washed off the table. She stripped the faded newspaper from the mantelpiece and gave the floor a second sweeping. Then she sat down on the side of the bed and rolled a cigarette and smoked a while, watching the blaze of the torch there in the fireplace. She finished one cigarette and rolled another. Then she undressed, washed her face and neck and arms, her arm pits, then her feet and legs and went to bed.

To-morrow was another day, and after that perhaps another. Just how long she would stay at Alex's, she didn't know. Perhaps a week, perhaps a month—maybe longer. She couldn't say. She liked Alex's.

CHAPTER V

Alex's house bordered the main road midway between Hannon and the Stand, and there was a frontage of some fifty yards or so that formed a sort of lawn between the house and the road. The Boro, where most of the farming arrangements were made, was ten miles farther on in a southeasterly direction. Plez Swanson's old shack, where Ollie was quartered, sat off to the right of Alex's house in the direction of the Stand. Knute Kelly and Bell lived in a two-room hut just beyond Ollie's, bordering the edge of a dense thicket, and they worked on a share-crop basis with Alex. Pink and her crowd lived across the road directly in front of Alex's, and Nan and Mae Jane occupied separate cabins some distance to the left, bordering the little red hill, on the Hannon end of the road. They, like Knute Kelly and Bell, were share croppers, working on a fifty-fifty basis with Alex.

The three men—Slaughter, Shell and Little Willie

—were quartered in a two-room, frame house that sat immediately to the left of Alex's. This house was constructed in much the same fashion as Alex's own. The two rooms were joined by an open hallway, and the kitchen butted the side of one room from the rear.

The three men occupied only one of these rooms. There were two beds, a table, three chairs, and such other household articles as were necessary for their simple needs. Shell and Willie slept in one bed and Slaughter occupied the other alone. Shell and Willie were brothers, the latter being the younger. Willie had just turned twenty when Ollie came to Alex's, a year older than Ollie herself. Slaughter and Shell were some years older, both of them being fully grown. So it wasn't strange that Willie was, in many ways, subject to the will of the other two. When there were extra chores to perform, such as drawing water, chopping firewood, or going for the cows of an evening, it fell to Willie's lot to do these things. He'd complain and frequently he and Shell would come to blows. But Willie would have to do them in the end.

68

Slaughter took no part in the disputes over such matters. He became active only when Shell and Willie lost their balance and threatened violence.

" 'Tain't no use you all fightin'," Slaughter would say then, thrusting his large frame between the two men. "You all is brothers! 'Side o' dat, Willie, you mought jes as well go on an' do it, 'cause you gwine do it anyhow."

"Aw, shut up!" Willie would retort angrily, glaring at Slaughter. And there the matter usually ended.

So this evening—the first day that Ollie had spent at Alex's—the three men had finished their supper, and now Slaughter and Shell were sitting by the fireplace, watching the blaze of the torch there. Willie was outside chopping kindling wood to keep the light going. There had been the usual encounter, but the incident had passed without serious mishap. Shell had slapped Willie and Willie had caught his older brother with a fast one to the chin, almost dropping him.

But Slaughter didn't move from his seat. It was the one incident among many, during which

Slaughter didn't appear to be interested in either physical violence or kindling wood. He sat with his elbows propped against his knees, his hands cupped about his chin, gazing intently at the fire. His eyes seemed fixed, the firelight mirrored in his eyeballs, like dancing flames in a crystal. Even when Willie sent his fist crashing into Shell's jaw, Slaughter continued to sit there. He seemed rooted to his chair by a force even more powerful than death itself.

So Shell and Willie were left to make their own truce as best they could. And when Willie finally went outside to do the chore, Shell turned to see Slaughter sitting there watching the blaze in the fireplace, as though nothing had happened. Shell pulled up a chair and sat down, but Slaughter didn't say anything. He continued to look at the fire and Shell rubbed his jaw with his fingers, watching Slaughter.

Finally, Shell said, "Whut's de matter wid you, boy?" Shell's tone was biting.

Slaughter said, "Nuthin'," and he didn't turn his

70

head. His eyes watched the fire, seemed glued there.

"Nuthin'?" Shell echoed.

"Dat's whut I said," Slaughter told him, without altering his tone. His voice was kind of sorrowful.

Shell said, "Oh," and looked at the fire, too.

Slaughter squirmed in his seat, took his hands from his face and gripped them together there between his knees. The pressure of his fingers made blue streaks on the surface of his skin, and the veins stood out beneath his flesh, at the junction of his wrists, like ribs in a sow's belly. He slumped further forward in his chair.

"Boy," Shell said now—and his tone was sympathetic—"I knows jes how you feel. A gal hit me lak dat once an' I ain't ovah hit yet. When a gal hit you in de right place hit's pure hell. Hit lak takin' a beatin' wid yo' hands tied behind you when you can't do nuthin' about hit."

Slaughter twisted again in his seat, leaned his head to one side and held it with his hand. He said, "Guess you knows whut you is talkin' about all right, 'cause I ain't nevah had no 'oman to do nuthin' lak dis to me before. 'Omans ain't nuthin' new to me. But last night when dis gal come in Uncle Alex's yard, look lak somethin' jes caught hold of me an' I couldn't move. An' dat ain't no lie—"

"I b'lieves whut you sey all right," Shell said, "'cause dis gal I knowed—"

"An' when we went to water de mules dis mornin'," Slaughter went on, "I tried to talk to her. Hit wa'n't dat I was tryin' to rush her or nuthin'. An' I wa'n't thinkin' about nuthin' dat was wrong. I jes wanted to be friendly-lak—sort of . . ."

Slaughter broke off, and Shell said, "I knows whut you mean. You jes wanted her to know dat you was thinkin' about her, an' dat whut you was thinkin' didn't mean nuthin' dat was wrong."

"Dat's right," Slaughter agreed, his eyes glowing fiercely. "Dat's whut I wanted to do. But she wouldn't give me a chance. Everything I sey to her, she sey somethin' right back at me jes lak she was cuttin' at somebody wid a razor. You know, she was kind o' easy-lak wid hit, lak she didn't want to hurt you or somethin'—an' cuttin' you all de time."

72

*"Boy," Shell Said Now—and His Tone
Was Sympathetic—"I Knows Jes How
You Feel. A Gal Hit Me Lak Dat
Once an' I Ain't Ovah Hit Yet.*

"Yeh," Shell said, "I could see de way she talk when you ast her 'bout goin' to de party. Her talk showed dat she got a heart on de inside o' her ribs lak a rock."

Slaughter sighed and said, "Ef she'd give me a chance, I'd be satisfied to marry her an' dat's somethin' I ain't nevah thought about doin' fer no 'oman. An' dat's de Lawd's truth!"

Shell said hopefully, "Mebbe she'll give you a play yet—you can't tell," and watched the torch burn down to the lower end of the kindling.

"Mebbe so," Slaughter said. "Mebbe she will—" His voice was a little sad, and his eyes, watching the slow-burning flame, were sadder still. The flame, consuming the last inch of fat pine, blinked out and flared up once—then went out completely. And the room was thick with darkness, save for the eerie, red glare of dying embers. The embers turned ashy and dead-looking, as the heat of the fire died within them. And the sound of Little Willie's ax, chopping more kindling wood, came through the walls of the house into the stillness there.

The two men didn't move. Neither did they speak. They simply sat there, half-staring and half-listening, as though held by something that neither of them could understand. Little Willie, whistling to the ring of his ax, was chopping kindling wood scarcely two feet from the outside doorsteps. . . .

When Willie entered the room, with a load of kindling in his arm, Slaughter and Shell were still sitting there and the fire had gone completely out.

"How come y'all set here an' let de light go out?" Willie said, and struck a match and set another torch upright in the fireplace. "Y'all jes want me to do evah—" He turned and saw Slaughter's and Shell's faces then.

Shell's mouth was half-opened, his lower lip hanging. Slaughter's face was hard, his jaws set, like an image cut in stone. Willie looked from Slaughter to Shell and then back to Slaughter again. Willie said feelingly, "Is you all fixin' to die?"

Slaughter twisted about in his seat, and Shell continued to look at the fire. Willie laid his hand on Shell's knee, shook him violently, and said: "Hey! Hey! . . . Wake up!"

76

Shell said, "Gawn an' leave me 'lone. You is jes a kid. You don't know nuthin'!"

"Don't know nuthin' about whut?" Willie said.

"Nuthin' about nuthin'," Shell said.

Willie stared at Shell, and Slaughter said, "Guess we bettah be goin' to de party, ef we is goin'," and lifted himself out of the chair. "Ain't no use to set here lak dis," he added tonelessly.

"Unless y'all is fixin' to die, hit ain't," Willie agreed.

"Aw, shut up!" Shell said, turning to Willie. "Ain't nobody fixin' to die. When you ain't knowed whut you is talkin' about, keep yo' mouth shut. Ain't gwine tell you dat no mo'!"

Willie grinned at Shell. He said, "You ain't no fool, Shell," and dry washed his hands with a brisk motion. He shifted his eyes back to Slaughter again, and his expression sobered. He watched Slaughter, as the latter pulled on his jumper and lifted the strap to his guitar over his shoulder. Slaughter's movements were slow and clumsy. But Willie didn't speak again. He turned and smothered the torch beneath the ashes. Then the three of them filed out of the room, Slaughter and Shell in the lead. . . .

Ollie had come to Alex's on a Monday, and a week from that following Saturday night she attended her first party at Lucy West's. Lucy lived on Phillpotts' place. Her two-room shack was perched upon a knoll across the road from Nan's house at the little red hill. One could sit on Nan's doorsteps and watch the "doings" there of a Saturday night. And this Nan usually did, for it provided her with choice and varied bits of news. And Nan liked news, choice or otherwise.

Ollie had gone to the party alone. Slaughter had offered to come by for her. But Ollie had said, "Nuh; no need to come by fer me. Ain't sho I is goin'. An' ef I does, I speck I'll go by myself."

So Ollie had gone, arriving a bit late after things were well under way. There had been a ball game and picnic at the Stand that afternoon, and the boys from Swanson's and Hannon stopped off at Lucy's to have a little fun before returning home.

The yard about the house was well populated

78

with both males and females when Ollie walked up. Slaughter and a man named Boto were making the music with two guitars. Slaughter played the lead part, while Boto added the musical trimmings in a bass tone. And they were breaking down into a fierce sweat now. It was one of those swampy blues pieces, whose words made little or no effort to shield their meaning, and whose music had a slow, artless way of suggesting things that the words might have overlooked. One understood the music completely. All one had to do was listen and keep shuffling. And they were shuffling now. With each vibration of the strings, their lithe, young bodies came closer together, as though harnessed by a fierce, compelling agony. Their laughing eyes were bright and sad-looking. Their faces were sad-looking, too. A liquor-like sadness, as though they knew not what they did—and cared less.

Ollie kicked off her shoes and shuffled in. And Little Willie caught her and drew her to him. Ollie heard music. Ollie felt rhythm. So Ollie was ready to go. Slaughter, from the seat where he sat, positively stared; and Willie grinned his surprise at his own boldness. Old men and young swung their partners about to get a look at this girl, and ladies from Black Bottom craned their neck and dilated their black, snapping eyes at the boldness of this creature's hips.

Ollie's eyes began to sparkle; her hair worked loose; and her body might have been one series of hips after another. For, now, it seemed jointless. It moved with a rhythm all its own.

Willie put his best foot forward, and around him her prancing took shape, and this boy began to feel the weight of his own importance. He could see Shell, standing there in the stag line, his red eyes staring, his hands doubled into fists and rammed into his pockets.

Willie swung Ollie around. The music got slower, each bass chord hitting a deeper note. And one by one the couples dropped out and gathered there in a semi-circle to watch this boy and girl strut. Hands and feet beat time to the music, and male voices got loud with praise. Once, a deep baritone whined, "Tell me, pretty mamma, where did you stay las' night? . . ."

The music ceased and Ollie sauntered over to a bench beneath an apple tree to catch her breath and mop her face. The night was hot. The air was still. And the moon glowed with a fierce, feverish brilliance.

Ollie sat down, and Willie leaned forward, his hand still in hers, and said: "I'd lak to hab the next dance too, Miss Ollie, ef you don't minds."

Ollie said, "I don't minds," and looked up at the boy's face and smiled. His face, she saw now, was radiant, his dark skin flushed with a strange warmth.

"You know, I likes dancin' with you," the boy said gleefully, releasing her hand and dropping into the seat beside her.

Ollie began rolling a cigarette. She said, "Oh, I ain't nuthin' much to brag about."

"Oh, yes'm you is, too!" Willie said. And the girl, glancing once again at his face, saw that his eyes danced. She went on rolling her cigarette.

Young men, minus their escorts, slipped off through the shadows and found their way to the bench where Ollie and Willie were sitting. Slaughter and Shell came, too. Slaughter's face was wet and smiling. Shell's hands were still buried deep in his pockets. He didn't look at Ollie. His eyes, the hot, reddish depth of them, were fixed on Willie.

The group stood there a moment, awkward and silent, and Ollie went on shaping her cigarette. Willie sat to one side in his seat, his left arm extended along the back of the bench, and watched Ollie. Watched the deft movements of her fingers and the bare, brown surface of her arms and throat, where the v-shaped neck of her waist came to a point at the junction of her breasts.

Slaughter pushed his way to the front of the group then, and said, "Thought you'd lak bein' here, Miss Ollie," and grinned.

"Hit's all right, I guess," Ollie said, glancing up with a slow movement of her eyes. Then she licked her cigarette and caught it fast between her lips. A man struck a match, dropped quickly to his knees, and held the flame to her cigarette for a light. But Ollie turned her head to one side, lit her own match, and said: "Thank you jes de same, mister, but I has my own matches."

"Sho she has," one of the others said loudly then,

"—an' she don't wants you lightin' no cig'ret fer her nohow. . . . Course she wouldn't mind ef it was me, 'cause she gwine give me de next dance anyhow —ain't you, Miss?"

"Who sey so?" the first man said, rising to his feet.

"I sey so—dat's who!" The man speaking was from Hannon, and his young adversary hailed from Swanson's.

Ollie took the cigarette from her lips, and said: " 'Tain't no use fer you all to start no fightin' about dancin' wid me."

But Ollie's words came a bit late. The man from Swanson's had passed the ugly word then, and the Hannon boy had flung it back into the other's teeth, neatly compounded, with the word "mother" preceding it. The Swanson boy buried his foot in the pit of the Hannon boy's stomach and whipped out his razor. The Hannon boy doubled over and played dead. Then he slid in under the Swanson boy's feet with a catlike movement and dropped him on his head.

They came to grips then, their muscles taut, their

83

bodies rigid, digging their bare fingers into each other's flesh. The razor was lying to one side there on the ground, where it had fallen from the Swanson boy's hand.

Slaughter stepped in and ripped the two men apart, and Lucy West herself shouldered her way through the crowd now, her eyes blazing.

Lucy said, "Who in de hell is dat tryin' to break up my party?"

"Dey was jes scrappin' a li'l bit, Aunt Lucy," Slaughter said. "But dey is all right now."

"Scrappin' a li'l my foot!" Lucy said. "Durn dey souls, ain't none o' dese black devils gwine break up my party!" She glared at the two men standing there, sweating and breathing hard, and said: "Now you two young niggers git you all's mules an' haul yo' rumps on away from here—dat's whut you all do. Now git—"

The two men slunk off and the crowd relaxed. Lucy stood there a moment, looking around. Then she spotted Ollie sitting there on the bench beside Willie, smoking a cigarette. Lucy smiled and said,

"Howdy do, daughter? Dem two fools musta been fightin' ovah you, wa'n't dey?"

"No'm," Ollie said, and smiled back. "Dey wa'n't fightin' ovah me."

"Now course dey was, daughter," Lucy teased, showing her bare gums in a broad, toothless grin. "Dem two bucks was gwine make hash out of one another jes to git de next dance wid you. You know, you is kind o' pretty-lookin', honey, an' de mens sho will fight ovah pretty 'omans."

"They was fightin' 'bout her, all right," somebody said.

"I knowed hit," Lucy said, "'cause dat's all de mens got to fight about anyhow—de 'omans."

"'Tain't no use to fight ovah me," Ollie said. "Peoples fight ovah somethin' they owns, an' when they don't owns nuthin' they ain't got nuthin' to fight about."

Lucy looked startled. She said, "Is you tryin' to tell me no man don't owns you, daughter?"

"No'm," Ollie said simply, "I ain't tryin' to tell you nuthin' lak dat. I was jes tryin' to sey they

85

didn't owns nuthin' fer as I was concerned. Dat was all."

Old Lucy savored this with a smack of her lips, but she didn't say anything. The men, huddled there, looked glum, and the women positively stared. Only Little Willie smiled to himself, sitting there beside Ollie, his elbows resting on his knees.

Lucy looked at Willie, and said, "Wonder whut dat li'l scamp see to be grinnin' about!" And a smile touched her lips now, made them seem oddly ridiculous, like those of a pouting child's.

"He ain't grinnin' 'bout nuthin', Aunt Lucy," Shell said bitterly. "Jes settin' dere grinnin' because he's a fool."

Willie went on smiling, and Lucy turned to Ollie and said, "Daughter, you come on back to de house wid me. I wants to ast you somethin' sort of privately-lak."

So Ollie followed Lucy to the house. Slaughter and Boto returned to their guitars and the dancing went on, it being just a little past midnight now. Willie remained seated on the bench and Shell stood there watching him, his eyes smoldering like hot embers.

When the others were safely out of hearing, Shell said, "You lay off dat gal, Willie—dat's whut you do! She's a grown 'oman an' you is jes a kid. 'Side o' dat, she ain't none o' you' kind. Don't aim to tell you dat no mo'!"

Willie didn't say anything. He didn't even look up. He simply sat there on the bench, his eyes watching the palms of his hands, his lips still smiling. He sat there a long time, picking at first this palm and then the other with his finger nails, as though Shell didn't exist at all

Then he looked up and saw Ollie standing in the doorway, with the firelight behind her, and he got up and walked back to the yard where the dancing was.

CHAPTER VI

OLLIE had followed Lucy back into the shed room the older woman used for a kitchen. The room was small, the floor fashioned from wide, thick planks, and the sides from unfinished pine boards.

Lucy closed the door that led into the main room and motioned Ollie to a low chair. "Take a seat, honey, an' make yo'self at home." Then she lowered her voice, and added: "I gwine give you somethin' to sort of wet yo' throat wid."

Ollie sat down and Lucy went to the back door to rinse two glasses. There were two demijohns on a bare, wooden table, with a corncob stopple rammed snugly down their throats. One bottle contained an inch or two of blackberry wine and the other was half filled with a clear, watery liquid. A copper kerosene lamp, with a round wick and no globe, shed a feeble, yellow glow for a light.

Lucy poured a sip of wine from the jug and

handed the glass to Ollie. "Bettah sort of let you taste it to see how you laks it first," Lucy said.

Ollie took a sip from the glass, smacked her lips slowly, and said, "Kind o' nice—only it's a little sweet-lak."

Lucy's face broke into a knowing grin. She said proudly, "Well, honey, ef dat'n is too sweet-lak, you try dis here jug. I keeps dis'n fer de mens, but ef you kin take whut's in hit—you is welcome to it, honey!"

Ollie uncorked the other bottle and poured an inch of the liquid in her glass and gulped it in two swallows. Then she stood there a moment, eyeing the glass soberly.

"Now dat's really nice," Ollie said.

"Dat's last year's corn," Lucy said, caressing the jug affectionately with her open palm.

"Hit's nice all right," Ollie repeated.

"Hit's kind o' tricky, too!" Lucy warned, dilating her eyes.

"But I laks de way hit goes down on de inside," Ollie explained, lifting the jug and pouring another half inch into the glass. "Hit's kind of smooth an' easy," she added, lifting the glass.

"Yeh," Lucy agreed, "hit's easy to take all right, but hit's kind o' hard to carry. Hit's got a kick to hit, lak a young mule!"

Ollie smiled. "Hit's s'pose to hab a kick to hit, Mis' Lucy," she said.

"Honey, don't I know hit!" Lucy countered warmly, and laughed heartily.

Ollie tilted her head back, and gulped once.

Then Lucy leaned suddenly closer, and said, "Daughter, what I wants to ast you is—is you done noticed dat Slaughter is natchl'y crazy 'bout you?"

"No'm," Ollie said, "I ain't noticed nuthin' lak dat." She looked directly at Lucy's face and eyes.

"Well, he is, honey," Lucy went on, " 'cause evah time he come up here, he be talkin' 'bout you— 'bout dat new gal whut Uncle Alex done hired!"

"I don't know zackly whut to sey 'bout dat," Ollie said, her eyes still regarding the older woman's steadily.

"Jes thought I'd mention hit, honey, dat's all," Lucy said quickly. " 'Cause after all, Slaughter is a good man. I means, he's so hard-workin' an' steady-lak. An' dem kind o' mens is hard to git dese days, 'specially wid all de triflin' ones around—"

"Yes'm," Ollie said. "But I guess—"

She broke off, staring at Lucy's face. Then she turned suddenly, and said: "Guess I'll hab to be goin' now. I promised Willie de next dance. Thank you fer yo'—yo'—"

"Don't mention hit, honey," Lucy said. "Won't you hab another li'l taste befo'e you go? Jes a li'l eye-opener, huh?"

"No'm," Ollie said. "Thank you jes de same." She moved through the door, and Lucy said: "Well, don't forgit dat li'l bug I done put in yo' ear, honey." But Ollie only smiled, and old Lucy stood there watching after the girl with a puzzled expression on her face.

"I don't know ef dat gal gwine lak Slaughter or no," Lucy told herself calmly, and poured a stiff drink in her own glass.

The party broke up early that Sunday morning. Slaughter and Boto had strummed piece after piece, and the dancing had gone on round after round. And each round, Ollie and Willie could be seen shuffling their way through the crowd. After each dance, the men would gather around Ollie to ask for the next dance. And each time, Ollie would only say, "Hit's done already been promised." And Willie would grin knowingly, and the next dance would proceed.

Ollie and Willie walked side by side going home, and Slaughter and Shell followed a few paces to the rear. Ollie didn't put on her shoes, once she was through dancing, but had tied the laces together and dropped them over her shoulder instead. The white sand was cool and deep, and the paleness of the moon upon it made the road seem strangely unreal, like a highway strewn with sugar.

Ollie walked with her head lowered, her eyes watching her bare toes, as they sank with each step into the cool, free earth. She didn't say anything, and Willie was silent. Dew had fallen and the air was cooler. She trudged along beside Willie, listening to the low mumble of Slaughter's and Shell's voices to the rear.

At Alex's, the two men turned off to go to their room, but Willie went on down the road with Ollie.

Shell paused and looked back at Willie. He said, "I gwine call dat fool. He goin' right on down de road wid dat gal!" But Slaughter said, "Don't call him, Shell. She don't mean nuthin' by lettin' him walk 'side o' her. She jes don't want to hurt his feelings by tellin' him she kin go home by herself— dat's all."

So Slaughter and Shell had gone to their room. But they didn't go immediately to bed. They sat there on the side of the beds, facing each other in the darkness, neither speaking. They sat there listening for the sound of Willie's footsteps, that would soon turn in from the road and come up the steps into the house.

But Willie didn't come. And so the two men continued to sit there, gazing across at each other, waiting and listening. Still, neither of them spoke and there wasn't a sound, save for the labor of their breathing. A half hour passed—then an hour. A rooster crowed, and now daylight began to creep through the cracks into the stillness there.

Shell said queerly, "Reckon whut's keepin' dat boy so long?"

"Dey musta got to talkin' about somethin', I guess," Slaughter said, without conviction. And once again there was silence. . . .

Ollie and Willie had walked slowly down the road until they came to the gap where Ollie usually turned in to go to her cabin. Here they paused and Ollie pulled a sack of tobacco from her bosom and began rolling a cigarette. Then she passed the bag to Willie, and said, "Won't you hab one?" It was plain that she was in no hurry to be gone.

Willie took the bag, and they stood there a moment, silently watching the moonlight, shaping their cigarettes.

Ollie said, "I don't feel much lak goin' to bed now. I ain't sleepy."

"Me neither," Willie said, and his eyes seemed to sparkle. The girl watched his eyes.

Ollie said now, "Guess there ain't no place to go though."

"Kin walk some," Willie said.

"Walk where?" Ollie said.

"Down de road—'cross de field—most any-where—"

Ollie turned her head slightly to one side. The moonlight, she saw, was soft and vivid—almost like day. And the surrounding fields, teeming with growing things, were lush and green and strangely alive now. Cotton and corn—green, growing, living things! . . . The girl's eyes were rapt with a kind of wonder, as though, looking at these things now, something deep within her had suddenly begun to ache.

She said, "All right, us kin walk some." And she turned to look at the side of Willie's face, a strange warmth filling her eyes.

They lit their cigarettes and walked on down the road in silence. Then they turned off to the left, climbed a steep embankment, and walked across an open pasture to a sparse thicket, where the earth made a gradual descent to the banks of an open stream.

Ollie led the way and Willie followed a pace or

96

two to the rear. The thicket was still, save for a
movement here and there in the branches above.
It smelled fresh and alive. The moon broke through
here and there to make queer, vivid patterns at their
feet. Now they ducked their heads to crawl under
branches that hung low against a sharp descent.
And, once, Ollie giggled when a brier caught and
held fast to the hem of her skirt, while Willie
struggled to release its hold. The brook made a
cool, liquid sound as they went steadily toward it.

Reaching the stream's edge, Willie paused and
propped one foot upon a log, and Ollie stood looking down at the dark blur of the water. They
stood thus for a moment, neither speaking. Then
Ollie turned, lifted her shoes from her shoulder and
dropped them to the ground. The earth here was
dry and firm and strangely free of vegetation. A
thin layer of pine needles covered it like a carpet.
Ollie sat down and the shadows of night seemed
to press in about her. She felt free and restless. Her
body felt restless. She leaned back till her head
touched the needles and her body lay flat against

97

the ground. She half closed her eyes, watched Willie, and listened to the water.

The boy stood with his back half turned. He hadn't moved. He stood, as if in a trance. His body, silhouetted against the semi-darkness, was slender and hard. Watching the lines of his body, the set of his flanks and shoulders, Ollie suddenly thought of Jule. Jule who was hard and lean like that from his hips up.

The girl stirred. She turned over on her side and drew her legs up tightly against the pit of her stomach. Then she stretched again, and lay perfectly still.

She said, "Willie?"

Willie jerked himself about. He said, "You call me?"

Ollie giggled softly. "Course I called you, Willie. Whut you standin' there dreamin' about?"

"Dreamin' 'bout nuthin'," Willie said. "Jes thinkin'."

"Thinking?"

"Yeh," Willie said, "thinkin' 'bout dat water. . . . Somethin' funny 'bout water—'bout de way hit

98

make you feel, when you hear de sound hit makes an' you can't see hit wid yo' eyes."

Ollie turned again, and was silent. She lay quite still now, watching the boy's face and eyes, as he stood there looking down at her. His eyes shone brightly. The flesh on his face seemed a little wet, as though the blood, surging hotly upwards, had flushed it. And Ollie reached up timidly and caught Willie by the arm and drew him down by her side.

They lay there a long time after that, scarcely breathing, with the sound of running branch water, like soft music, in their ears.

Day was just beginning to break then. . . .

CHAPTER VII

It was good daylight when Willie crept quietly into the room. Shell, lying fully clothed across the bed, drew himself up with a start. He looked at Willie out of sleepy, red eyes; and when he spoke his voice sounded thick and uncertain.

Shell said, "Whur you been, boy?"

Willie looked at Shell and grinned. "Jes been tendin' to my business, Mister Shell," he said, and stripped off his jumper and hung it on a nail.

Slaughter, aroused now, sat up suddenly straight, and Shell got to his feet. Shell's eyes didn't leave Willie's face.

Shell said now, "Is you been wid dat gal all dis time?" The words fairly leaped from his lips.

Willie had dropped his suspenders and was unbuttoning the front of his shirt to slip it over his head. He didn't stop; neither did he speak. He finished with the buttons, reached his arms backwards over his head and caught the tail of his shirt, and slipped his head free.

Shell caught him and pinned him against the wall then, while Willie's arms were still bound up in the sleeves of his shirt. Willie, caught off his guard, gave little resistance, and Shell twisted the shirt to form a knot about the boy's wrists and arms, tying them up completely. Shell worked his free hand into the collar of Willie's undershirt, holding him against the wall, his knee pressed firmly against the boy's stomach.

Slaughter didn't move. Just sat there on the side of the bed, as though paralyzed by what he saw.

"Guess you kin answer me now," Shell blurted out, breathing hard. "Ef you don't, I gwine kill you! Kill you dead, you hear?"

"I ain't gwine answer nuthin'," Willie said. "Git yo' knee out o' my stomach!"

"You been wid dat gal, ain't you?" Shell said.

"Git yo' knee out o' my stomach," Willie repeated.

"You been to her room!" Shell went on. "You follow her—"

102

"You ain't gwine pick me," Willie said. "Git yo' damn knee out o' my—"

Shell applied more pressure, and Willie tried to free himself by inching sideways along the wall.

Shell said, "I give you one mo' chance! . . . Is you been wid dat gal, or ain't you?" His voice rose sharply with a thick, cracking sound, and Willie gritted his teeth and inched further along the wall.

"I told you to lay off'n dat gal, didn't I?" Shell was saying. "I told you she was none of yo' kind. An' den—den—you go on an' dance wid her an' follow her yonder to dat shack. An' now—now you come sneakin' in here dis time of mornin'—lak—lak you was—"

Willie said, "You a lie!" and buried his teeth in the fat of Shell's neck, and followed him into a heap there on the floor.

Shell's hold was broken. Willie ripped his arms free and they came to grips on an equal footing.

Slaughter was on his feet now. He lifted Willie bodily from Shell's midsection and stood the two boys apart at arm's length.

"No need fer dat now, y'all," Slaughter said. "No need fer hit at all!"

Shell glared at Willie, his neck and mouth bleeding. He said, "I ruther see you dead! I ruther see my ownself dead!" And his voice sounded shrill and helpless, like a woman's.

Willie turned and sat down on the side of the bed, exhausted. Slaughter released his grip on Shell, then turned and sat down beside Willie, his elbows resting on his knees, his eyes on the floor. Shell continued to glare at Willie, his eyes burning. But Willie leaned back on his elbows and stared straight ahead. A ray of sunlight slanted in through a crack, and outside the gentle peace of a Sabbath morning was broken only by the cackle of fowl and the distant lowing of a cow.

For a time, the three men remained silent, as though caught up by the simple realism of their own thoughts. Of the three, Willie seemed the least affected by this sudden turn of events. He simply relaxed, staring straight ahead. Slaughter, on the other hand, in spite of Shell's outburst, appeared to be the most vitally concerned. He sat there on

104

the side of the bed looking at the floor. And he seemed hurt, like a man who had once had hopes.

Slaughter sighed and shook his head. He glanced sideways at Willie reclining there on the bed, with his body bare from the waist up. He said, "You an' Mis' Ollie musta stopped down dere an' talked a while, didn't you all, Willie?"

His voice sounded queer and flat.

"Yeh," Willie said. "Us talked a while."

Slaughter breathed easier. He said, "Whut did you all do then?" and looked at the floor.

"Us walked some," Willie said.

"Walked?"

"Yeh," Willie said. "Walked."

"Walked where?" Slaughter said.

"Down de road."

"Den—den you all didn't go to her—her house?" Slaughter caught his breath and held it. His face was wet.

"Nuh," Willie said, in the same flat tone, "us didn't go to her house. Hit wa'n't no need."

Slaughter dropped his head and looked at the

floor again. He continued to look at the floor a long time.

Willie got up, finished undressing, and crawled into bed. And, presently, he slept. He had hoped for nothing and had received far more than he had dared to expect.

Shell's position, on the other hand, was strangely different from that of either Slaughter's or Willie's. He wasn't moved by any desire for Ollie himself, and his real concern for Willie was more of resentment than otherwise. Willie was only a boy—not yet fully grown. This fact was important to Shell. And this girl, even though she were young, was a woman. Besides, Shell knew of Slaughter's feelings for Ollie. Slaughter had told him and he had understood. Shell could sympathize with Slaughter. Slaughter was grown.

Willie began to snore now, breathing deep and fast. But Slaughter and Shell continued to sit there, as though they were still waiting for something.

Slaughter stood up and began pulling off his clothes mechanically. Then he paused and looked down at Shell. He said, "You don't reckon her an' Willie—you don't reckon they—"

Shell twisted uneasily. He said, "Dat's jes whut I was fixin' to ast you. Hit's somethin' dat I wants to know an' don't wants to know, both at de same time. Ef I could know, without knowin' dat I knows hit, dat would make hit easy. I could go to sleep an' wake up feelin' de same as I was before I went to sleep. But lak hit is now, I wants to know an' can't know. An' dat's de part dat hurts you."

"But you don't reckon dat she'd do somethin' lak dat jes to be doin' hit, do you?" Slaughter said. "I mean she—she wouldn't do hit without habin' some reason—somethin' in de back o' her mind?"

"A 'oman kin want a man, can't she?" Shell said. "She kin want him de same as he kin want her, can't she?"

"Den you mean she—she jes natch'ly wanted—Willie?" Slaughter said.

"Dat's de only way I kin figger hit," Shell said, "ef hit's true."

Slaughter was silent. He unbuttoned another

button on his shirt, then stood there without moving, the sound of Willie's breathing in his ears. He said, "Yeh; I guess you is right." He spoke as one speaks in a trance. Then he pulled off his clothes and crawled into bed.

CHAPTER VIII

The week beginning that Monday was in the teeth of the growing season. Corn was knee high and cotton began taking on stature by leaps and bounds. The weather was fine. June nights were short and hot. June days were long and hotter still. Cotton weather. Short hot nights and long hot days! Field hands had to work cotton fast.

From dawn to dusk, man and beast had to sweat, plowing and hoeing. When the plowing was caught up, plow hands took over a hoe. Mules went to pasture and man and woman had to sweat alone. From sun to sun, from Monday morning to Saturday noon! Saturday afternoons they went to ball games and picnics. Saturday nights they went to frolics. And on Sundays there was church. They had to go to church. They couldn't sweat and sin the week long for nothing.

Came July and August and the sweet scent of

cotton blossoms. Green corn stood tall and proud in silk and tassel. Plowing and hoeing ceased. Crops were laid by and field hands took their ease. Watermelons were ripe; late July days were long and lazy; and sin became a thriving, living thing. It was so easy to sin and eat watermelons and pray for forgiveness. There was nothing else to do. Field hands went to bed late and got up early. Field hands were people. They breathed, had longings, and went about with a curious ache, that was a kind of poetry, locked within the confines of their souls. So they had to do something.

August faded quickly and September slipped quietly in, turning the green leaf of summer to a rich gold. Work was plentiful again, gathering the harvest, and life stood still. The harvest was ripe and mellow. It was as if the fierce heat of Summer, when green things fought to live and grow, had suddenly cooled with the spent warmth of its own passion. And brown hands and bent bodies went about plucking the fruits thereof with a merry content. They gathered and filled their storehouses and cribs, and considered the fruits of their labor as blessings. They prayed not with sadness, but gave thanks with joy. A prayer was a song; a sigh was a curse. So they picked cotton and sang. They pulled fodder and let out whoops and field cries. What was work and sweat when you could sing— and, singing, your soul, your very being, ceased to live and began to soar? . . .

Ollie, beginning her third week at Alex's, settled easily into the leisurely routine of hoeing and plowing. She went forth early when the dew was heavy and returned late when the dusk was thick. Work and sweat and the heat of day gave her little concern. She was born to work. Throughout June and July she plowed and hoed. She gave a hand to the milking, and on rainy days she helped Caroline around the kitchen and with the wash. Saturday afternoons and evenings, she went out for a little pleasure. On Sundays, she went to church. It was as simple as that, week in and week out. And when the crops were laid by, she took her ease until the fodder was ready and cotton stood white and glistening in the sun.

But existence for this girl didn't end there. Nan,

for one, saw to that. And, of course, there was Jule.
Always Jule! And now Slaughter and Little Willie.
But Nan . . .

That Monday morning, following Ollie's first visit
to Lucy West's, Nan was down to the yard before
daybreak. She had got Mae Jane out of bed on her
way down. Milking the cows and getting them to
pasture was Nan's chore. But milking wasn't the
sole concern of Nan this particular morning.

It was barely daylight when Nan entered
Caroline's kitchen, with Mae Jane at her heels.
Alex was seated at the table sipping coffee from a
saucer, the warm vapor steaming fresh and fragrant
from his lips.

Nan said, " 'Bout dat gal, Alex—dat Ollie Miss.
She ain't fit—"

Alex said calmly, "Morning, Nan!" and he didn't
lift his eyes from the saucer between his fingers.

"I done speak a'ready," Nan said. "Clean yo'
ears out, Alex. Clean 'em out!" Nan's voice was
loud.

"Didn't hear you," Alex said, his voice still calm.
Then he lifted his eyes and added: "Morning, Mae

Nan Said, " 'Bout Dat Gal,—Dat Ollie
Miss, She Ain't Fit—"

Jane." The latter was just entering the kitchen now.

"Didn't hear me!" Nan said, drowning out Mae Jane's greeting entirely. "Well, you gwine hear whut I gwine sey 'bout dis gal. You gwine hear it, Alex, 'cause dat gal ain't fit to stay on dis place. She ain't fit—you hear dat?"

"Ain't ask you ef she's fit, is I?" Alex said.

"Don't need to ast me," Nan countered, " 'cause dat hussy was up to Lucy West's house Saddy night. Up dere dancin' an' friskin' herself right in front o' dat low class o' niggers from Hannon yonder. Prancin' an' twistin' herself wid dem mens lookin' right smack at her! . . . And den dey gits to fightin' an' carryin' on—wanting to cut one 'nuther throats ovah dat gal. I could see'm. I was settin' right dere on my porch, watching. An' dere it was Sunday mornin' an' her up dere friskin' herself lak she was a bitch dog."

"Didn't nobody git kilt, did they?" Alex said.

"Dat ain't de p'int!" Nan said sharply. "Dat ain't de—"

"What's the p'int then?" Alex said, and continued to sip his coffee.

Nan's breathing rose sharply and the muscles along the sides of her face twitched. Her pinched-up face seemed to grow narrow and draw up, and the flesh around her eyes and at the corners of her mouth screwed itself into tight little knots. Her bosom began to heave. She continued to stare at Alex, her eyes blazing.

Nan said, "Dat heifer ain't gwine stay on dis place, dat's de p'int!"

Alex drained his saucer and settled it gently on the table. He said evenly, "Bettah tend to yo' milking, Nan. You is pretty good at milking."

Caroline came in from the smokehouse then. Caroline was carrying a side of meat in one hand and a stone jug filled with sorghum in the other. Monday morning breakfast. Caroline was in a hurry.

Caroline said, "Mornin', Nan; mornin', Mae Jane," and hurried on by. Mae Jane returned the greeting meekly, but Nan didn't say anything.

Caroline placed the meat and the jug on the table. Then she turned and looked at Nan, at the side of Nan's face as she stood there glaring down at Alex. Caroline said gently, "Whut's de matter, Nan?"

"De matter?" Nan's eyes snapped, and Caroline shrank back a little. Nan's face began to sweat. "Ain't I done jes git through tellin' Alex," Nan went on, " 'bout de way dat Ollie Miss been carryin' on yonder at Lucy West's house last Saddy night? An' ain't Alex done jes as good as tell me, settin' right dere in dat chair, dat hit ain't none o' my business?"

"Now, Nan," Caroline pleaded, "you all go on an' git de milkin' done so Alex kin git de plows goin'. Dis is Monday mornin', Nan!"

"Monday mornin' my foot!" Nan said. "I ain't gwine a step tell Alex sey whut he gwine do 'bout dis gal!"

"But, Nan, honey," Caroline said, "ain't you knowed dat Alex can't sey whut de gal kin an' can't do, 'specially when de gal is grown an' workin' fer her own livin' an' kin go an' come when she please? Alex don't mind whut de gal do long as she don't do nuthin' wrong while she's here—"

"He gwine mind whut she do," Nan said.

117

A silence fell then, thick and soundless, and Alex got to his feet. But before he could speak, Ollie appeared in the doorway and the silence endured.

Ollie said, "Good mornin', you all. How you all dis mornin'?"

Caroline and Mae Jane said, "Mornin', daughter," and Alex spoke warmly enough. But Nan said, "Gal, wa'n't you up to dat party at Lucy West's house Saddy night?"

"Yes'm, I was dere, Mis' Nan," Ollie said, mounting the steps slowly, her eyes regarding Nan's intently.

"An' you was up dere friskin' yo'self, too, wa'n't you? Up dere wallowin' around wid dem mens?"

"Yes'm—" The girl checked herself. "Yes'm, I danced a li'l, ef dat's whut you mean, Mis' Nan," she finished, and her eyes didn't leave Nan's face.

Nan breathed deeply. She said, "Well, who was dat low-down scamp you was dancin' wid?"

The girl hesitated and looked at Alex. She said, "Oh, dat was Willie."

"Willie who?" Nan's eyes glowed hotly.

"Li'l Willie whut—whut stays here."

118

"You is a lie! You is—"

Alex took Nan by the arm and pushed her before him down the steps, and said, "You kin milk the cows, Nan, an' tend to yo' business. Or you kin git yo' things together an' move!"

Nan looked at Alex kind of hard then. She looked frightened and a bit helpless. All the fury within her seemed to well up into her eyes, and her eyes became glassy and red, like balls of fire, and tears began to roll down her face. She seemed bewildered, like a child. And her eyes seemed stark and wasted, too, with the water seeping from under her lids and spilling over on her cheekbones. Then her tears dried up, leaving her eyes naked in their sockets; and she didn't make a sound, save for that queer hissing at the intake of her breathing.

Nan turned and went swiftly through a hot Summer's dawn towards the lot, where the cows waited to be milked, Mae Jane at her heels. And Alex turned and went slowly back up the steps and into the kitchen.

Caroline said, "You hadn't ought to speak to Nan lak dat, Alex. Nan don't aim to—"

"Ought to tend to her business, then," Alex said shortly. He picked up his hat and went out into the soft morning's air.

When Alex was safely out of hearing, Caroline turned to Ollie and said, "Honey, you hab to 'low fer Nan when she start takin' on lak dat. Nan— Nan ain't got no husband. Nan ain't had no husband since she was a young 'oman. Nan's husband tuck an' walked off an' left her, an' all dese years, Nan ain't knowed whut to hab a husband was lak. . . . You see, honey, hit sort o' made Nan—hit sort o' made her . . ."

Caroline's voice trailed off and Ollie stood there, full-bodied and strong, gazing out into the fresh warmth of Summer. And it kept running through her mind, like a refrain: "Mis' Nan ain't got no husband . . . an' all dese years Mis' Nan ain't knowed whut to hab a husband was lak. . . ."

CHAPTER IX

Throughout June and July, Ollie went about her task and Nan was silent. But if Alex's attitude stayed the lash of Nan's tongue, it didn't seem to lessen the intensity of her curiosity. Day in and day out, Nan watched Ollie—watched her movements, the places she went and, as far as this was humanly possible, the things the girl did and said. And once Nan's anger had had a chance to cool, she began to consider more carefully the admission that Ollie had made concerning Willie and the party at Lucy's. Ollie, Nan had felt then, was trying to hide something—make it appear less ugly by saying that she had danced with Willie, rather than admit that it had been "one o' dem low-down niggers from Hannon yonder."

But one noon, as the plow hands came in from the field, Nan had observed that Ollie and Willie rode side by side. They talked, appeared to share some secret between them, for now and then their teeth would flash in a broad smile. And this seemed to Nan a little odd. Had it been either Slaughter or Shell, she'd probably have overlooked the incident entirely. Besides, Nan had heard it whispered that Slaughter was rather taken with Ollie himself. But both Slaughter and Shell, Nan saw now, brought up the rear, for Shell was plowing old Tom. Alex had made the switch. Alex had said, "You bettah take the cow, Shell. Can't let Willie plow up every other row o' cotton. No need to plant cotton jes to git it plowed up. No need at all—"

So Shell took old Tom and Willie plowed Queen. And this noon, Nan stood there by the well and watched Ollie and Willie ride in from the field.

At the lot gate, Ollie slid down from her mule and Willie took the reins of both animals and led them inside to the stalls. Ollie, Nan saw, didn't go inside to help with the feeding as she usually did. She stood there by the gate and waited until Willie came out. Then they walked together to the house, their lips moving in low speech, while Slaughter and Shell tended their share of the feeding.

Nan observed this with a set look in her eyes.

122

And that evening, when the hands came in for the night, she called to Willie and said, "Willie, when you is done wid yo' feedin'—come here to de cow pen. I gwine git you to help me do something."

"Yes'm, Mis' Nan," Willie said. And when he had finished with the feeding, he went into the cows' pen and Ollie proceeded on her way to the house alone.

Nan said, "Jes want you to help me part dese ol' cows an' calves, Willie. Mae Jane done had to go on to de house yonder wid de milk. Only take a minute."

"Yes'm," Willie said.

Then Nan coughed and said, "Sey, Willie, you was up to Lucy West's party t'other Saddy night, wa'n't you?" Nan said it casually, as though it didn't matter in the least.

"Yes'm," Willie said, "I was dere all right, Mis' Nan."

Willie grinned and Nan could see the gleeful look that lit up his face and eyes. Nan watched his eyes.

"Well, who did you dance wid, Willie?" Nan

123

said then, heading off a calf, "Sook, sook—sook dere!"

"Who, me?" Willie said. "Oh, I was dancin' wid Mis' Ollie! . . . Me an' her—us was de main one—"

"But she dance wid some o' de others, didn't she?" Nan shot the boy a quick look.

"No'm," Willie said. "She ain't dance wid nobody but me. Me an' her—us dance together all de time us was dere. Dem others! . . . No'm, Mis' Nan, she lak dancin' wid me!"

Willie's grin broadened and Nan could see the pride of the young male swelling within him. The boy's eyes glowed richly, the whites forming crisp half moons in the settling dusk. For an instant, Nan didn't speak. She stood there and watched the boy's face; watched that strange, hot eagerness that glowed there. Nan could see there was something deeper behind that look than just dancing. And she watched Willie now, with her mouth half opened, as though she had become a little greedy to know just what that something was.

Nan turned to one side to spit. Then she said,

124

"Reckon dat's 'bout all, Willie. An' thank you fer helpin' me wid dese ol' cows an' things."

"You sho is welcome, Mis' Nan," the boy said proudly. Then he added: "You know, Mis' Nan, Mis' Ollie kin sho-nuff dance some, too. Whut I means, she kin sho-nuff strut some—"

"Kin she?" Nan said, and paused, a sly grin creasing her lips. "Don't reckon she let you take her home after de dance or nuthin' lak dat, did she?"

"Oh, yes'm, she did, too," Willie said. "Yes'm!
. . . An' den—den me an' her—us tuck an'—"

Willie checked himself and looked up to see that greedy look on Nan's face. Nan's eyes were like a cat's eyes.

"You an' her tuck an' done whut?" Nan said eagerly. "What was you fixin' to sey, Willie?" Nan's eyes glowed, but her voice was gentle and pleading.

Willie said, "I was jes fixin' to say us—us tuck an' walked on down de road to de gap where Mis' Ollie turnt off to go to her house. Dat was all, Mis' Nan." Then he turned and went swiftly up the path to the house.

Nan continued to stand there with her mouth

125

half opened. Then she closed it and said half to herself: "De lying young scamp! De lying young dog! . . . An' Alex gwine let dat young heifer run loose on dis place! . . ."

The first few weeks following Lucy's party Slaughter lapsed into a strange silence. He didn't sulk. Merely he seemed baffled, as though his feelings for this girl had become so pronounced that he was at a loss to know how to proceed. Actually, she filled his thoughts during every minute of the day, and far into the night. Whenever she spoke to Willie, or smiled at some casual rejoinder from the boy, Slaughter's face would tighten and begin to sweat. Somehow he seemed helpless, as though his own feelings made him helpless.

But at night, when Willie wasn't around, he'd talk to Shell. Again and again, they'd go over the events of that Sunday morning following Lucy's party, and each time the whole affair would appear even more mystifying than before.

"Hit ain't dat I blames Willie," Slaughter would

say. "But ef I could jes know how hit all happened! Ef I could jes—"

Slaughter would break off and clinch his fists, and Shell would say bitterly: "He done hit on purpose! I told him to lay off'n dat gal!"

"But mebbe hit wa'n't Willie's fault," Slaughter would say then.

"He made a play fer her yonder at de party, didn't he?" Shell would retort. "He kept on—"

"But she didn't hab to dance wid Willie ef she didn't want to," Slaughter would remind him plaintively. "An' she didn't hab to let Willie walk home wid her neither, ef she didn't want to."

Shell would sit there then and look dumbly at the blazing torch in the fireplace, his breathing swelling in the pit of his throat, and his body would begin to tremble. Once he said hotly, "I know whut I gwine do! I gwine tell Uncle Alex! No need to let dat boy make a fool out o' hisself ovah dat gal!"

Slaughter had turned to look at Shell then, and his eyes seemed frightened. He said, "Don't do dat, Shell. Don't sey nuthin' to Uncle Alex!" He said it so sharply that Shell, turning to look at the tenseness in Slaughter's face and eyes, felt the natural sweat turn cold on his brow.

"You see, hit ain't Willie," Slaughter had gone on. "Hit ain't whut her an' Willie done done. Dat don't matter."

Slaughter paused and swallowed hard, and his eyes seemed to merge and shrink away, like headlights seen through a depth of water.

"Ain't Uncle Alex gwine find out anyhow?" Shell said. "Ain't he gwine see'm slippin' around?"

Slaughter sighed, and when he spoke again, his voice was scarcely more than a whisper.

"Hit ain't dat, Shell. Willie, he don't matter. Whut Uncle Alex gwine see don't matter neither. Hit's—hit's jes somethin' I feels."

It was no use. He couldn't quite say it. Slaughter could see that now. It was like seeing a thing across a perilous depth, reaching for it, and yet not being quite able to reach it. It managed somehow to elude his grasp, and he'd shrink back, frightened. And Slaughter could see himself crouching there, hoping eventually to grasp that something—feel himself clutch it. And yet there was that in the look on his face which seemed to know that he never would. Not quite.

So night after night, Slaughter would sit and talk to Shell, and he was never quite able to say the thing that he wanted to say. Probably he didn't know how to say it, or just what it was that he wanted to say. Probably he only felt it, the way a man feels that he wants a woman without knowing why.

Then he'd stand up and roll a cigarette, walk over to the window and stand there a while, drawing the smoke deeply into his lungs, and gaze starkly out into the night. Then he'd return to his chair and sink down, and he and Shell would continue to sit there and watch the blazing torch, until Willie would come in.

CHAPTER X

OLLIE left Alex's place for the first time on a Friday night. It was the middle of July and the crops were laid by. Ollie told Alex she'd be gone for a few days. "Jes feel lak visitin' fer a spell," Ollie said. "Fer 'bout a week." And Alex agreed.

"It's all right, Ollie," Alex said. "Works is 'bout caught up, an' we won't start pullin' fodder for another two weeks. Aim to be back to help out gatherin' th' crops, don't you?"

"Sho, I aims to be back all right," Ollie told him.

Ollie met Alex coming out of the lot gate that evening, on her way to help Nan and Mae Jane milk the cows. Her eyes were deeply set and her voice rang with an eager tenseness. Her face glowed, as if her going held for her a definite mission.

Alex let his eyes rest soberly upon the girl's face, but he only said, "Guess you is kind of lonesome. Hope you have a good time while you is gone."

131

He paused, then added: "Need any money to help you along?"

"Thank you, Uncle Alex," Ollie said, "but I don't reckon I needs no money or nuthin' lak dat. Don't aim to buy nuthin' whilst I is gone, an' I kin always git somethin' to eat. Thank you jes de same."

"All right then," Alex said. "So long."

"So long, Uncle Alex," Ollie said.

And that was all. Alex didn't ask where she was going or why. Had he asked, Ollie would have told him. She would have said, "Jes goin' to see a friend of mine, Uncle Alex. His name is—is Jule." But Alex didn't ask and Ollie didn't say. She went on around to the cows' pen to do her milking, and Alex went up the trail to the house. . . .

Outside of her cabin, Ollie hunched the bundle farther upon her shoulder with a lurch. A breeze was blowing, but it was warm and smelled of rain. The sky was black and low, and the darkness bulked before her eyes and swallowed her. It was going to rain. She could hear the deep murmur of the swamp, the distant croak of water frogs. The wind was beginning to change, and it whipped the side of her face now.

She cut across a cotton field, skirted the hog wallow, and went through the bottom. Her strides were measured. Turning into the swamp, the air felt suddenly still and damp. She unbuttoned her jumper and slipped the cloth from about her neck, and mopped her face. Now and again she felt the sweat drip from the point of her chin and trickle down between her breasts. It had begun to drizzle.

An owl hooted in the distance, and a frog heaved its body into a puddle of water at her approach. The rain fell steadily now. It sank through to her skin and mingled with the sweat on her body. She shifted the bundle to her left shoulder and rolled a cigarette, her legs holding their pace. She lit the cigarette, inhaled deeply, and watched the trail rush toward her and disappear beneath her feet.

Her clothes got wetter and the trail grew sloppy. Tiny specks of mud splashed against her thighs and dried into tight, itchy crusts there against her flesh. The rain beat down against her face, and into the gap, where the jumper fitted loosely about her neck.

She scarcely felt it now. Her legs kept moving, and she peered soberly into the darkness and listened to the rain. It fell in soft singing sounds upon wet leaves and the spacious swamp. The sounds fascinated her, and she went down the trail and through the swamp, as though she walked in a dream. She forgot about the rain. She forgot herself. And the only living thing she could think about now was Jule. She was going to Jule! She hadn't seen Jule for eight weeks.

She thought about the morning, years before, when she had gone to the cornfield to cut green corn for the livestock. Old Duck had sent her. It was July and the feedstuff was low. A Summer's sun stood red and blistering in a milky sky. Now and then a breath of air stirred, touched the blades of corn, making a soft din about her ears, like rain on dripping leaves. She was sixteen then.

She worked one row down and started another coming back, chopping each stalk at the root with a jut of her hoe. Then she sat down in the shade of a corn middle to cool off and mop her face.

It was while sitting there that she first saw Jule.

134

He was leaning against a snag scarcely a rod away, his hands doubled into fists and rammed awkwardly into his pockets. She didn't know how long he had been standing there. His eyes watched her intently, as though fascinated by something strange and unearthly. His body was big and strong, and the muscles on his arms showed huge ripples, like a giant's, where his sleeves fell short.

She sat there a moment, watching his arms, but she didn't say anything. Then Jule began walking toward her, and she had a feeling that his arms could squeeze and crush every bone in her.

Ollie stood up. Jule came close to her and stopped, but he didn't say anything. Only his eyes spoke. They were still and luminous now, like slow-burning white flames, pouring back into her own the spark of something sweet and eternal; and she knew then that he looked upon her as a woman.

Jule touched her hand and then her cheek. His fingers felt hot, and her body trembled to the touch. She caught hold of him to steady herself, and her body went closer to his. Their faces touched, and she felt his arms tighten about her waist. The

135

breeze stirred again, and the fodder began to sing; and she knew something within her was trembling and crying. . . .

After that she saw Jule almost every day. He lived on the Wright place across the creek, and he was two years older than herself. Sometimes they met in the cornfield, and sometimes Jule came to the house where she lived. Once her Aunt Duck had caught them in the corn crib, with the door shut, and old Duck had whipped Ollie. She whipped her with the clothes peeled from her back. She would have whipped Jule too, if she could have caught him.

"I ain't fixin' to give you dis beatin' 'cause you done sin, gal," old Duck said. "I is beatin' you to keep you from sinnin'."

"But us wa'n't doin' nuthin', A'nt Duck," Ollie said. "Us was jes settin' in dere talkin'—wasn't us, Jule?"

"Us sho' wuz, Mis' Duck," Jule said. "Jes settin' in dere talkin' an' lookin' at one another."

"Yeh, you all was jes settin' in dere talkin' all

right," old Duck said. "But I gwine fix hit so you won't set in no crib an' talk wid de door shut."

Jule set out to running then, but Ollie didn't move. And that made old Duck angrier still.

"Gal, you done got so bold you figger you is grown! You ain't eben scared of no beatin' no mo!"

The rawhide left welts on Ollie's back, but she didn't whimper. She merely stood there with her head bowed. And the next morning when Duck woke up, Ollie was gone, and her clothes were missing. She and Jule went to the Crossroads to live! . . .

Ollie hummed softly under her breath as she moved deeper and deeper in the swamp. The cigarette had burned short and died a wet butt between her lips. The rain had turned to a fine, misty fog now, and toward the east luminous splotches of gray marked the rising of a late moon. She felt tired, but her feet kept moving. She shifted the bundle to rest her shoulder; and once her voice broke a piercing bleat upon the night:

137

Ollie Miss

Day done broke,
Lawd, de sun done riz;
Hit's time to go home
Po' boy . . .

CHAPTER XI

J UST before daybreak, Ollie was standing on Jule's doorstep, tired and exhausted. The clothes on her back were sticking to her skin, and her breath was coming fast. She caught her breath deeply and knocked once. But there was no answer. She knocked again, her face pressed against the door, listening. And still there wasn't a sound.

She straightened, reached her arm through the slit between the logs and released the chain, and went in.

The cabin was in shadows. Three-legged skillets stood on the hearth before the fireplace. The bed showed signs of use, but was unmade. Jule, she saw, still lived there, but he wasn't home. She said aloud, "I come to see Jule!" She said it as though she had never thought of the reason why she had come.

She stood there in the middle of the floor, letting

her eyes rove about the room. A pair of overalls and a shirt—Jule's clothes—hung on a nail against the wall. She walked over to the nail and took the shirt and overalls in her hand, and dropped her bundle. She'd change to something dry, build a fire, and sit down to wait. She felt tired and hungry, but she'd wait. She had come to see Jule, and being tired and hungry didn't matter now. After she had seen Jule, she could rest and sleep then. Sleep would come easy, and food—even dry bread and water—would possess the natural sweetness of milk and honey.

Ollie changed to the overalls and shirt, built a fire, and sat down in a chair to wait. Day was beginning to break, and now and then she'd turn her head to look at the door, as though she expected to see Jule standing there, tall and straight, looking down at her—his eyes going straight through her. Jule would know why she had come. She wouldn't need to explain that to Jule. She had never had to explain that to him.

His body would sway a little as he moved toward

140

her. He wouldn't smile or say anything. He'd just walk over to her chair and stand there, looking down at her, as if he hated her for coming. But he wouldn't hate her, and his eyes wouldn't leave her. They'd seep into her and go all through her, and her body would begin to feel a little weak. She'd rise from her seat to meet the challenge in his eyes, and her head would drop against his shoulder, and her eyes would smart and grow a little wet.

Ollie dropped another piece of kindling on the fire and watched it burn slowly down, and her legs and body felt a little stiff. Her eyes felt tight and heavy. She fixed her eyes on the blazing torch to keep them open. She didn't turn her head to look at the door now. Just watched the torch. The flames flashed red and blue streaks before her eyes, and her head seemed to turn slowly, around and around. But she continued to sit there, watching and waiting for Jule! . . .

Ollie slept, sitting there before the fireplace, clothed in a pair of overalls and a blue shirt.

When she opened her eyes, the sun was shining. The cabin about her was bright with daylight, and Jule hadn't come. She stared about the cabin, then stood up, her joints feeling cramped. She stretched and was suddenly conscious of the emptiness in the pit of her stomach.

She set to work, building a fire. Then she found water in a bucket on the table and washed her face. There was meal in a tin, a side of meat in a box of salt, and a demijohn half filled with syrup. Jule's victuals. She said half aloud, "Wonder how come Jule didn't come home?"

Then she thought of Della—Della who had furnished Jule this cabin to live in. Della had asked Jule to marry her, but Jule wouldn't. Then she had asked Jule to come and live with her, but Jule wouldn't do that either. So she had given Jule this cabin to live in so he'd be near her. She offered Jule money, and wanted to buy his food and clothes. But Jule wouldn't take Della's money, and he worked for his own living. That is, he used to. Ollie didn't know what he was doing now.

She stirred up the meal with water and salt, adding the grease from the fat bacon for seasoning. And a thought struck her. She'd go over to Della's house as soon as she finished her meal. Maybe Jule had stayed there last night.

Ollie dropped to her knees before the fireplace and forked the meat, crisp and brown, out of the skillet. She poured her bread into the skillet, covered it over, and heaped hot coals upon the lead top so it would brown. Then she stood up and looked around the room.

The sun, blazing through the cracks in the roof, revealed the dirt there on the floor. "Guess I'll clean up a bit for Jule," she said, and turned and walked over to the bed and stood there a moment. The quilts and sheets, she saw, were dirty and in a jumble. "Guess Jule ain't had no time to think about cleanin' up or nuthin' lak dat," she said, and tugged at the end of a quilt, turning it over. And her eyes saw something. She picked the thing up between her thumb and forefinger, and looked at it. It was a slip, but it didn't belong to Della. The size of it told Ollie that. It was slender and narrow through the

143

waist, and pretty. She looked at the garment, then at the bed, and smelled her bread burning.

She swung around and dropped to her knees before the fireplace, and drew the skillet back and lifted the lid. The top crust was scorched a little, but the bottom was a rich, golden brown. The smell of it made her mouth water.

She turned the bread out on a plate and cut it in quarters. Then she noticed the garment still in her hand, and the sight of it made her a little sick. She dropped it on the fire, holding it out from her between her thumb and forefinger. Then she sat down and ate her meal in silence. Sorghum, meat, bread, and sweetened water. She chewed and swallowed her food, as though she didn't feel it at all.

CHAPTER XII

"I HARDLY evah see Jule any more," Della said. "He go off an' stay fer weeks at a time, an' sometime when he be comin' in late at night he mought stop by. But he don't loose no mo' time wid me. Peoples say he go yonder to Roba and Fort Davis an' places lak dat. They sey he got a new 'oman dere. They sey she jes a young gal an' sort o' pretty-lookin'. They sey her an' Jule done fell in love wid one 'nother an' they is gwine git married. . . ."

Della's voice died away. She looked up at Ollie's face beseechingly, and her lower lip quivered. And, for once, Ollie looked as though she could feel sorry for Della—Della who had caused her and Jule to break off.

Ollie breathed a sigh and brushed the ash from her cigarette. She didn't say anything. She simply looked at Della's face and the swelling about her eyes.

They were sitting in Della's doorway, facing each other in the settling dusk. They had sat there every evening since Ollie came, talking and looking down the trail toward the swamp, each hoping in her own way that Jule would come. Ollie had made the trip especially to see Jule, and the knowledge of another woman didn't matter now. She simply wanted to see Jule. To-day was Friday and to-morrow she was going back to Alex's.

With Della, it was different. Della wanted Jule to come while Ollie was there. Della felt that, if Jule would come now and see Ollie, she could get a new hold on Jule herself. Della despised Ollie—despised her very insides. But she saw in Ollie's presence now her only hope of getting even a partial grip on Jule. Men, Della felt, were sometimes like that. When they had pie they wanted cake. They didn't know why they wanted pie and cake, both at the same time. But they did. And when there wasn't any more pie they didn't want the cake. They wanted something else, even though that something might be slop. So, when Ollie was around, Jule would come to her. He'd pay her some

146

attention, spend an evening or sit awhile. But after Ollie left, Jule didn't come around her at all. And that hurt Della. It hurt her and puzzled her, too. It increased her bitterness against Ollie. Della didn't know that, while Ollie was around, Jule would come to her simply because his going back to Ollie would be the sweeter then. Jule could appreciate Ollie after Della. That Della, herself, had never mattered, Della was never to know.

So, now, they sat there—Ollie and Della—in Della's doorway and talked. And now and then each of them would look down the trail as far as the eye could see, as though they hoped to see Jule, tall and strong, emerging from the maze of a settling dusk, coming home to his own! . . .

They had sat there every evening since Monday and now it was Friday. And Jule never came. But they continued to sit there and wait, speaking now and then a word to break the silence, only to fall silent again. And sitting thus, side by side, staring into the dusk and waiting for Jule, they seemed closer to each other than they had ever seemed be-

147

fore. They seemed almost like sisters, with but a single, redeeming passion to mark their sisterhood.

That first morning when Ollie came over from Jule's cabin, Della was stooped over the fire preparing her breakfast. Seeing Ollie standing there in her doorway, Della had looked up startled, and for an instant she didn't speak. Only the rhythmic rise and fall of her breasts, with a single cotton garment drawn tightly about them to shield their bigness, revealed the tension of life that still coursed, lush and full, through her body.

Ollie said, "How you, Della?" She said it simply, letting her eyes go swiftly about the room.

Della continued to stand there in a half-crouching posture. Then, seeing the look in Ollie's eyes, she straightened and said, "Oh, he ain't heah!" and laughed hysterically. She stopped suddenly and pulled her dress together in front, for the safety pin that held it together across her bosom had snapped. She looked at Ollie soberly. She said, "You lookin' fer Jule?" She said it twice, with a touch of bitterness in her voice. And when Ollie didn't answer, she added: "Well, he ain't heah! I ain't got him in my li'l pocket dis time—"

Della threw her head back and started to laugh again, but Ollie said quietly, "I already knows dat, Della," and drew her cigarette tobacco from her bosom and began rolling a cigarette.

Della sobered again, fixed Ollie with her eyes, and said, "Whut you mean—you already know?" Della took a step forward, her bosom heaving.

Ollie glanced up at Della's face, but she didn't say anything. She went on shaping her cigarette and watching that queer, eager look on Della's face. And when she struck the match and held the flame to the tip of her cigarette, she thought of the tiny garment she had found in Jule's bed that morning. She could see it now, as she had held it between her thumb and forefinger, just before dropping it on the fire. And looking at Della, Ollie wondered how much larger that slip would have to be before Della could even work it up over her hips.

Ollie said, "I jes sort o' figgered he wouldn't be here—dat's all, Della," and turned to flip the match stem through the door out into the yard.

Della's lower lip dropped, quivered. She said, "You been by Jule's already?" She spoke as though she wanted to cry.

"Yeh," Ollie said matter-of-factly, her eyes still on Della's face. "Stayed dere last night."

"An' Jule nevah come home?"

Ollie shook her head, and Della said, "Oh, Lawdy!" and drew her dress so tightly across her bosom that the flesh stood out beneath it, like ribs.

Della turned and walked back to the fireplace and pulled the skillets back from the fire and sat down in a chair. She sat there with her arms folded across her lap and her shoulders began to heave, huge drops of water rolling down her face. Crying made Della look old and helpless and starved. And Della was a fat woman.

Ollie said, " 'Tain't no use to cry, Della. Ain't nuthin' to cry about."

Della looked up at Ollie, her eyes blazing through her tears. She bounced to her feet and said through clinched teeth, "You evil, black bitch, you! You tuck an' worked a spell on Jule! You done him somethin' to make him hate me! . . . Git out o' my house! Git—"

Ollie watched Della without moving, the cigarette caught between her lips. But before she could speak, Della dropped to her knees and clung to Ollie, her upturned face tearful and pleading. Della's face seemed suddenly fleshless and she began to whine like a child. She said hysterically, "Don't go, Ollie—don't pay me no mind! I didn't aim to sey dat. Honest, I didn't, Ollie! 'Clare 'fore God, I didn't! . . . Hit—hit— Somethin' tuck an' made me sey dat, Ollie—"

Ollie looked at Della, and still she didn't say anything. She simply took Della's arms from around her and stood the whole two hundred and ten pounds of Della on her feet.

Della shivered. She pleaded, "You gwine stay heah wid me, Ollie? You gwine stay heah tell Jule come back? . . . Don't go! Don't left me heah by myself tell Jule come! . . . Mebbe—mebbe ef Jule come back an' see you—mebbe . . ."

So Ollie stayed and Della told her all about the new girl that Jule was in love with yonder at Roba.

"I nevah lay eyes on her or nuthin'," Della said one evening, as they sat there in the doorway. "An' ef I does, I gwine rip her heart out o' her bosom. Lawdy, ef dat hussy would jes git up de nerve to come out heah an' spend one night wid Jule! . . . Jes one night, Lawd—dat's all I ast! . . ."

Ollie looked straight into Della's mouth when she said that, but she made no reply. She simply leaned back against the door facing, took a long draft on her cigarette, and fixed her eyes on a point far out into the distance, where the soft purple of night merged with the jet blackness on the swamp. She sat there drawing the smoke deeply into the recesses of her soul, as though she might be dreaming. And Della went on mumbling, her voice coming and going, like the rise and fall of a swishing tide.

Ollie left Della's just before sundown that Saturday evening. She stayed at Della's all day Saturday. But Jule didn't come. So she knotted her bundle to her wrist and set out for Alex's.

Della had prepared a lunch for Ollie, but at the last minute she tried to persuade Ollie to stay over until Sunday.

"Dis is Saddy night," Della pleaded, "an' Jule mought be comin' out to git fresh clothes. He mought stop by on de way to his shack." But Ollie said, "Nuh, I guess I won't stay. Reckon I bettah git back so I kin rest up fer Monday. Fodder mought be ready to start pullin' den."

So Ollie went up the little trail, passed Jule's cabin, and skirted the edge of a cotton field and entered the swamp. Just before she dropped out of sight, she looked back to see Della still standing there in the doorway. Della's bulk seemed pitifully small at a distance. It seemed like a round, fat doll, lost and bewildered.

The swamp was a flame of color against the setting sun. Ollie entered it and began thinking about Jule—about Jule and Della and herself. This other girl didn't matter now. Just thinking of Jule, of the fact that she wanted to see Jule, made Ollie want to live. It gave her something to live for. But Della? What about Della?

Ollie didn't know about Della. All she saw was the fleshy bulk that had once been Della Dole,

153

standing there in the doorway, as though it were a statue—something fixed and dead, lifeless. . . .

It seemed sort of queer to Ollie. It seemed like a riddle.

CHAPTER XIII

W<small>HEN</small> Caroline opened her kitchen door the next morning, Ollie was sitting on the crosspiece, swinging her bare legs in the dewy air. Caroline said, "When you git back, honey?"

"Las' night," Ollie said.

"It musta been kind o' late, wa'n't it?"

"Yes'm," Ollie said. "After midnight."

"Well, daughter, ain't you scared to be trampin' up an' down dese swamps after midnight by yo'-self?"

"No'm," Ollie said. "Ain't nuthin' gwine bother me."

"But you is a gal, honey!" Caroline said.

"Dat don't make no dif'ence, Mis' Ca'line," Ollie said.

"But s'pose somethin' happen to you? S'pose—"

"Ain't nuthin' gwine happen," Ollie said.

"But, honey"—Caroline's voice dropped to a whis-

155

per—"you mought meet up wid some o' dese stray mens prowlin' around. You mought—mought be comin' up here wid—wid—"

"Peoples don't hab babies less'n dey want 'em, Mis' Ca'line," Ollie said simply, and Caroline looked startled. Caroline said, "Lawd hab mussy, Jesus!" and turned around as if to go back into the kitchen. But she didn't go. She said, "Daughter, don't you know whut you is sayin' is a sin before God? An' don't you know you'll go plum to hell fer messin' around wid God's business?"

"Yes'm; dat's whut I hear evahbody sey, Mis' Ca'line," Ollie said. "But, den, mebbe de Lawd is worryin' mostly 'bout de people's souls. Mebbe de Lawd ain't got time to think about somethin' lak dat."

"Well, Jesus—" Caroline checked herself and stared at the girl sitting there on the crosspiece, swinging her bare, bright legs. Then she said in a different tone, "Ollie, honey, come on an' eat yo' breakfast so you kin help Nan and Mae Jane milk de cows. An' you pray sometimes, you hear? Git down on yo' knees an' pray! Pray real hard. Pray tell you can't pray no mo'—"

156

"Yes'm," said Ollie, "but I sey my prayers evah night 'fore I goes to bed, Mis' Ca'line."

Ollie went in the kitchen and ate her breakfast. Then she picked up two milk pails and went out the back door. Willie was drawing a bucket of water at the well as she went down the steps. Ollie spoke to Willie and stood there a moment talking to him in low tones. Then she went through the gate towards the lot.

That Monday morning, following Ollie's departure for Jule's cabin, Nan had a talk with Slaughter and Shell. The two men were working around the lot that morning, cleaning out the stalls, since there wasn't any work to be done in the field. Willie was helping Mae Jane drive the cows to pasture, and this gave Nan an opportunity to talk to Slaughter and Shell alone.

So, when Nan had finished her milking, she went inside the lot to the stalls where the two men were busy raking manure into piles, before wheeling it out to dump it into a neutral corner against the lot fence.

Nan said from the doorway, "I see you all's buddy done left fer a spell—huh, Slaughter?"

Slaughter looked up from his rake at Nan's face, and Shell said loudly, "She ain't no buddy o' mine, Mis' Nan."

Nan greeted this with a smile, and Slaughter didn't say anything. Nan looked at Slaughter—then at Shell.

Nan said, "Well, how come she ain't no buddy o' your'n, Shell?"

"Jes 'cause she ain't," Shell said, and his eyes flashed a rich, flaming red.

Slaughter spoke for the first time then, and said, "Mis' Ollie ain't sey how long she gwine be gone, did she, Mis' Nan?"

"Nuh; she ain't sey how long she gwine be gone or nuthin' lak dat, Slaughter. Jes picked up her bundle an' walked off! . . . Course you all know 'bout de dancin' her an' Willie tuck an' done yonder at dat party de other Saddy night, don't you?"

Slaughter looked at Shell and Shell looked at Nan. Shell said, "Us sho do, Mis' Nan—'cause us was right dere."

158

"An' her an' Willie dance toget'er all de time they was dere, didn't they?" Nan said.

It was Shell's turn to look at Slaughter, and Slaughter said, "Not de whole time, Mis' Nan."

"They was dancin' evah time I seen 'em," Shell said, and his tone was edged with bitterness. He glanced quickly at Slaughter's face, and then toward Nan's again.

"An' Willie tuck an' walked home wid her, too, didn't he?"

"Yes'm; her an' him walked on down de road toget'er," Shell said.

"Did Willie sey ef he went all de way to her—her house?" Nan asked.

"Jes sey they walked on down de road a piece," Shell said, and wet his lips. "Down to where—"

"An' did Willie come right on back soon as he git down dere?" Nan went on. "Or did he stay down dere a while?"

"They stood down dere in de big road an' smoked a while," Slaughter put in. "Jes smoked an' talked— dat was all dey done, Mis' Nan."

159

"Is dat whut Willie sey?" Nan was looking at Shell.

"He ain't sey nuthin' about no smokin', Mis' Nan," Shell said, and Nan's eyes widened. Slaughter looked at the ground, and began raking manure again.

Then Nan said, "'Bout how long you all figger Willie stayed down dere?"

Neither Slaughter nor Shell spoke, and Nan said, "You all wa'n't in bed when Willie come back, was you all?"

"Willie nevah stayed down dere no long time or nuthin' lak dat," Slaughter said, and beads of sweat dripped from his forehead.

Shell looked at Slaughter and then at Nan. He looked at the nakedness in Nan's eyes and caught his breath on a lengthening note.

Nan scarcely breathed at all. She fixed Slaughter with a direct stab of her eyes, and said, "'Bout how long you figger it was den, Slaughter, before Willie come back? . . . 'Bout a hour? Hour an' a ha'f—or—"

"It wa'n't no long time, Mis' Nan," Slaughter re-

160

peated, and streams of sweat began trickling down the sides of his face. "Let's see—I figger mebbe it was 'bout—"

Slaughter paused to wipe his face. And Nan looked quickly at Shell, and said, "How long you figger it was, Shell?"

"It was good daylight when Willie come in," Shell said. "I knows dat much, Mis' Nan, 'cause me an' Slaughter done set dere on de side o' de bed waitin' fer Willie. An' when Willie nevah come right on back, us fell off to sleep wid our clothes on. An' when Willie come creepin' in dere, it was broad open daytime an' de sun was shinin'.'"

Nan grinned broadly at this, as though it were only a joke. Then she looked innocently at Slaughter, and said, "Guess you all kin finish you all's work now, Slaughter. Didn't mean to stop you all from workin'. Jes stopped to sey dat Ollie is done gone trampin' fer a spell. Jes figgered you all mought want to know."

Nan smiled again, as though it were still only a joke. Then she turned and walked out of the lot, and Slaughter and Shell stood there gazing at each other in the silence that followed.

When Nan was out of hearing, Slaughter said, "No need to tell her how long Willie stay down dere wid Mis' Ollie, Shell."

"She ast fer it, didn't she?" Shell said defensively. "An' all I done was to tell her de truth, ain't it?"

"De truth don't matter," Slaughter snapped, and his voice trembled. "It was none o' her business. She was jes pickin' you to find out somethin'."

"But she tuck an' ast fer it," Shell repeated. And, once again, there was silence.

Shell went on raking manure into neat, brown little piles, and Slaughter stood there looking at the ground.

Slaughter was standing at the lot gate as Ollie came down the path with two milk pails in her hand. He had a stack of green corn on his shoulder he had cut for the mules' feed. He had got up early that Sunday morning to help Alex with the feeding, since Alex had to drive to Hannon to meet the new preacher. And seeing Ollie, as she came slowly

162

down the path, Slaughter stood the corn against the fence and waited.

The girl's approach was leisurely, her eyes averted. And when she came in speaking distance, Slaughter said, "Mornin', Mis' Ollie. Heard you went visitin' fer a li'l while."

"Yeh," Ollie said. "Went to see a friend o' mine. . . . How is Slaughter?"

"Pretty good," Slaughter said. "Hab a nice time?"

"Pretty nice," Ollie said simply.

Slaughter looked at the ground, and his lips tightened. He said quietly, "I was sort o' waitin' to tell you somethin', Mis' Ollie. Somethin' I figgered you'd want to know."

Ollie said, "Whut about?"

Slaughter shifted uneasily. He said, "It's—it's 'bout you and Willie. It's—" He broke off, and added with a sigh: "Ain't much, I don't guess. Jes somethin' I figgered on tellin' you when you hab a li'l time to listen an' nobody is around."

The man stopped speaking, but Ollie didn't take her eyes from his face. She looked at his face, as though she felt that she had been unfair to him in a

163

way she hadn't intended to be. Finally, she said, "Any time you feel lak tellin' me whut you got to sey, it's all right wid me."

"Ef you is goin' to church," Slaughter said hopefully, "I kin tell you den."

"I jes seen Willie at de yard," Ollie said, releasing her gaze, "an he ast me to go 'long wid him. So I don't reckon dere'll be no chance to talk den."

Slaughter stood silent for a moment, as though turning this over in his mind. Then he shifted awkwardly again, and said, "Oh, Willie done already ast you?" He spoke as though the full import of the girl's words had just then taken root in his mind.

Ollie said, "Yeh; he done already ast me," and turned to move toward the gate that led into the tie-up where Nan and Mae Jane were milking.

Slaughter wheeled quickly and said, "Mis' Ollie, ef you kin come back down to de lot after you git through milkin', I kin tell you den. I gwine stay down here tell de mules git through eatin' an' hitch up de wagon."

"All right, I'll come back," Ollie said. . . .

164

"It was Mis' Nan," Slaughter told Ollie later, as she stood with her back against the crib door, smoking a cigarette. "She was astin' questions 'bout you an' Willie. She was talkin' to me an' Shell dere in de stable one day. She was astin' us how long Willie stayed down dere wid you de night he walked home wid you from Aunt Lucy's party. She was astin' us ef it was a long time an' whut Willie sey when he come back. She wanted to know ef Willie sey he went to yo' house an'—an' ef you all dance together all de time you all was at de party. She was astin' dem things, Mis' Ollie, lak she was tryin' to find out something—lak as ef she done had some reason fer astin'. It wa'n't so much whut she was sayin' as it was de way she was sayin' it. So I jes figgered I'd tell you 'bout it so . . ."

Slaughter stopped speaking and the girl dropped her cigarette to the ground. She caught her breath slowly, and said, "I is kind o' sorry Mis' Nan bothered you an' Shell 'bout something you all ain't knowed much about. Ef Mis' Nan had ast me in de first place, mebbe I could of told her something she mought hab been glad to hear. Fer dat reason, I is

165

sorry, 'cause whut I mought hab sed mought hab been de same as ef Mis' Nan done seen it wid her own eyes."

Ollie stood there a moment looking at the ground. Then she looked up at Slaughter's face, and said, "Thank you jes de same," and went slowly back up the path to the house.

Slaughter turned with a sigh and put the mules in harness and drove the wagon up to the yard and stopped it at the front gate. The hands would gather there and take their places in the wagon before the drive to church. Caroline, Nan, Mae Jane, Knute Kelly and Bell. Ollie and Willie would come on behind, walking side by side in the middle of the big road, and he and Shell would be sitting side by side on the driver's seat.

Slaughter sighed again, sitting there in the empty wagon, watching the lazy motion of the mules' tails against the doubletree. "Guess I shouldn't hab told her dat," he said softly.

CHAPTER XIV

$\mathbb{T}$HE camp meeting got under way late in September. Cotton picking was practically at an end and seed money was plentiful, the harvest drawing swiftly to a close. Late September nights were lazy and warm. The moon was full. Field hands flocked to the meeting on foot, in wagons, on horseback, in buggies, and moved about the churchyard in thick, boisterous huddles. Their talk was loud and merry, and their laughter throbbed with a brittle sadness.

Ollie went to the church each night alone. She'd set out on the mile walk through the moonlit stillness, after the wagon with the refreshments and the other hands had departed. At sundown, the mules were fed and the wagon was hitched, and usually Slaughter or Shell did the driving. Once, Slaughter had said, "Hit'd be nice ef you'd ride up in de wagon toget'er." But Ollie shook her head. "I kind o' likes to walk," was all that she said. And once, too, Willie hung around long after the others departed. But Ollie made it plain that she preferred to go alone.

"Sometimes I jes feels like walkin' by myse'f," she told Willie. "Jes feels like walkin' an' sort o' lookin' at de peoples an' things when dere ain't nobody else around."

So, each night, the girl went up the road alone, trudging slowly through the deep white sand, with the fierce brilliance of the moon about her.

The church was visible from the crest of a hill a quarter of a mile away, its bright, whitewashed walls beaming proudly in their lush green setting of oak and poplar. It was a squat, boxlike building with a mere runt of a steeple, and it crouched low over stubs of brick-red pillars, like a tiny hen mothering its brood.

The trees fringed hedgelike about it, forming a dappled, moonlit grove. And toward its outer edge, the grove petered out to mere clumps of pine and cedar saplings, to which saddle horses and mare mules were tethered and left to stand. But nearer

168

the church, temporary stands stood in thick clusters, like circus booths, among the trees.

Ollie could see the stands now. Kerosene lamps blinked, and men with sweaty faces pumped their arms furiously, waving lanterns and beckoning to the crowd to sell their wares. Their voices sounded hoarse and thick and a little strained in the distance, and now and then dog horns and cow bells took up the call.

Entering the grove, Ollie shouldered her way leisurely through the crowd, sniffing the smell of fresh fish sizzling in hot grease over open fires. Here and there voices called out, "Hey, Ollie!" or "Dere goes Ollie Miss!" And somewhere the strings of a guitar throbbed lazily, the heavier ones talking bass talk, like a natural man. Now and again a voice would cut in and pick up the tune, chant it moodily, with the same lazy, half-crazed rhythm:

> *"Lawdy Lawd—*
> *Look where de sun done gone,*
> *De sun done gone . . ."*

Ollie moved on. The crowd swarmed and frolicked, white shirts clinging to sweaty, sticky bodies.

"Barbecue an' fresh lemonade, five c-e-n-t-s!"

That was Uncle Alex. Ollie could see his thickset frame, perched on a box, waving his hat and calling out to the crowd. His voice rose in hoarse whispers now, and sweat trickled down the sides of his face and dripped from the point of his chin.

People milled about Uncle Alex's stand, nudging and inching their way to the narrow wooden counter. Once there, they took a glass of lemonade in one hand and a barbecue sandwich in the other, dropped two nickels or a ten-cent piece, then backed away to eat and drink in loud, laughing groups. Married women pranced and giggled. Single ladies rolled and snapped their bright, black eyes with delicious winks. And men, both married and single, shuffled in and mingled among them, squeezing their arms and whispering knowingly into their ears, only to receive, in return, a playful little push in the face.

"Gawn, you ol' bull!" a deep contralto would retort, teasingly. "I ain't none o' yo' wife."

Teeth flashed and lips smiled, and heavy laughter floated darkly upon the night. . . .

"Barbecue an' fresh lemonade, fi—"

Ollie moved on and guitar music went on throbbing. The crowd surged back and forth in thickening streams, going from stand to stand and through the grove, and out by the well, then down the lane and around a bend to the sweetgum tree. Over a white sandy hill, there were willow trees and a frog pond. But couples weren't headed that way as yet. They simply moved about the grounds in squads, or groups of a dozen and a half dozen. Laughing and joking, whispering and giggling. Male and female.

Ollie circled through the crowd and went past the well and headed down the lane, spotting here and there the faces of people she had come to know. There were Uncle Len and old Hamp. Uncle Len hobbled about munching barbecue and playfully patting the younger women from behind, on a spot he had no business. Then he'd cup his fist about

a listening female ear and whisper something and
wheel around, shuffling off quickly at a dogtrot, and
cackling his own loud belly whoop amid shrieks of
laughter.

But old Hamp merely stood there, knock-kneed
and quiet-like, his lips peeled back from his gums,
snickering softly through his nose. Even in the
dimly illumined shadows, one could see his swollen,
blood-red gums, the worn stubs of his teeth set in
them like tiny, yellow pegs. Now and again he'd
sniff the air sharply, and say: "Dese young pullets
sho' do smells good!"

Ollie saw Cora and Folks Wright standing in the
center of a small group, as she went on down the
lane. Folks had a dingy, mud-yellow face that
screwed itself into knotty wrinkles about his eyes
whenever he grinned. And Folks was always grinning. He was grinning now, with one hand jug-
gling a buggy whip and the other encircling Cora's
waist, patting her gently—almost affectionately.
Ollie had heard people say that Folks would beat
that whip to a frazzle over Cora's back the moment
he got mad. And once, it was told, he had crowned

Cora with a singletree when he came in from the field and found his victuals weren't cooked.

But, now, there they were: Folks grinning and Cora standing proudly by his side, eating a fish sandwich and sipping lemonade, as though he had never struck her a lick. People said that Cora was a fool,—that she didn't have the sense she ought to have been born with,—staying yonder in that house with Folks, cooking his victuals and washing his clothes, and he right regularly beating on her, as if she might be a dog or something.

Ollie looked at Cora quite frankly for a moment, at the pathetic sag that had begun to pinch the corners of her mouth. Then she glanced once again at Folks, standing there with that buggy whip in his hand, and moved on down the lane. She picked up her feet and set them down a bit queerly, flat on their heels, her eyes watching a sea of shiny, laughing faces with long direct stares, as though she didn't see them at all. . . .

"Barbecue an' fresh—"

Mar Moore's wife and Cæsar were coming up the lane, arm in arm, as Ollie went around the bend toward the sweetgum tree. Mar Moore had gone up North yonder to work, leaving Daisy there to gather in the meager crop of cotton and corn. Nan and Mae Jane had said that Mar Moore was a fool, the same as Cora was—only a bigger one! Going off yonder and leaving Daisy there by herself when Cæsar was around!

"Ain't Sis' Frances' gal, Birch," Nan had pointed out, "who is ol' enough to know bettah done had two chilluns fer dat Cæsar? An' ain't Cæsar done been sweet on Daisy, eben befo'e her an' Mar done git married?"

"He sho' is now," Mae Jane had said.

Ollie caught a fleeting glimpse of Daisy's eyes as she passed. Daisy's eyes were bright and kind of wet-looking, and she went on giggling softly and pressing her body closer to Cæsar's. "Us is goin' in de church sho' nuff to-night when de meetin' start, ain't us, honey?" Daisy said, teasingly.

But Ollie didn't hear what Cæsar said. She went on down the lane and turned up the road by the sweetgum tree, and her body was trembling. She kept remembering that look in Daisy's eyes, with the moon shining full on them, and thinking about what Nan and Mae Jane had said about Birch and Cæsar, and about Mar Moore and Daisy. But the things that Nan and Mae Jane had said didn't seem to matter now. Cæsar and Daisy's husband didn't seem to matter either. But that look in Daisy's eyes —the same look that must've been in Birch's eyes when—

Ollie had walked far up the road, almost half way to the Stand, before she realized the distance she had traveled. She paused and sat down on a log lying there beside the road and gazed off into the white, silent night. The road was deserted and still, and she sat there half listening to the sounds that drifted out from the churchyard, like the rumble of distant thunder. She sat there a long time, just looking, as though her mind and body had become a bit numb.

Then she stood up and said aloud, "I guess Jule ain't heard nuthin' 'bout no camp meetin' up dis fer."

Then she turned and walked slowly back down the road toward the church.

175

When Ollie got back to the sweetgum tree, she could hear the singing. The meeting had started and people were closing up their stands and going into the church now. Couples climbed down out of buggies, or drifted from behind tree trunks where they had been standing, and strolled out of the grove, going either to the church or walking arm in arm out toward the frog pond and willow trees. They couldn't loiter about the churchyard while the services were going on. They either had to get off the grounds or go inside to the meeting.

Ollie stood there in the shadow of the sweetgum, leaning against its huge trunk. Couples kept coming out of the grove and groups of men could be seen moving through the shadows in back of the church, heading toward the graveyard. The men in groups wore overalls and caps pulled low over their eyes. There weren't any women among them —just men, their feet moving in a slippery, shuffling walk. Now and then a group would pause in the shadow of a tree, and Ollie could see a flat bottle passing from mouth to mouth, when a match flared to light a cigarette.

176

Ollie was still standing there by the sweetgum when Willie turned the bend coming down the lane. The boy's face glistened in the moonlight, and his feet dipped forward with long, rambling strides. He came directly to the tree where Ollie stood, his lips smiling.

"I been lookin' fer you, Mis' Ollie," he whispered, and his eyes lit up.

"I was jes walkin' around an' now I is on my way back up to de church," Ollie said, and looked at his eyes. "Ain't you goin' in to hear de meetin'?"

"No'm." Willie grinned and his eyes sparkled. He took a step closer to the girl. "Figgered me an' you could walk some," he went on, "ef I could find you."

He stood there, breathing heavily, looking at Ollie. Ollie didn't move. She watched his face with listless, sad eyes.

"I—I guess I don't feel like walkin' no more now," she said.

"Jes a li'l ways," the boy urged. "Den—den us could set down an' rest some fer a while."

"Not dis time, I don't guess, Willie!"—simply.

177

Ollie stood up suddenly straight and glanced away. She hesitated, looked once again at the boy's face, and Willie shifted uneasily in his tracks. His face looked hurt and his eyes had lost their luster. He said, "Couldn't us jes—jes be toget'er fer a li'l while?" His voice sounded thick, trembled.

Ollie shook her head, but her eyes didn't leave his face. She said, "No, Willie—not to-night." She took a deep breath and went slowly up the lane toward the church.

The last of the couples came straggling out of the grove now, as the church marshal went searching among the trees with a buggy whip in his hand. And Ollie went on up the lane and passed the well, and the singing kept getting louder. It sounded queer and sweet, that singing. It sounded as though the people were marching and singing all at the same time, with Gus Ellison carrying the lead.

"Lord, I felt like shoutin'—
When I come out de Wilderness,
Come out de Wilderness,
Come out de Wilderness.

*Ollie Went Up the Steps and Slipped
Into a Seat Just Inside of the Door*

Ollie Miss

> *"Lord, I felt like shoutin'—*
> *When I come out de Wilderness,*
> *Leanin' on de Lord . . ."*

Ollie went up the steps and slipped into a seat just inside of the door. People were patting their feet and the church seemed to rock. Gus Ellison kept walking up and down in front of the rostrum, with his eyes closed and his head thrown back, his arms swinging out and around and dipping to the swing of the music. The singing got louder still, then died away to a whisper. The church began to moan, and Gus Ellison folded his arms and went down on his knees. Ollie bowed her head and sat there and listened. . . .

CHAPTER XV

I<small>T</small> was Wednesday, the third night of the meeting. People began to arrive in fresh droves from Roba and Magnolia, from Creek Stand and Swanson's, from Hannon and Gerrington and points farther south. The news had begun to spread. Distant travelers brought quilts in their buggies and mattresses in their wagons, with enough corn and fodder to feed their livestock the remainder of the week. They came to frolic and to see things and to hear Gospel preaching. The grove about the churchyard throbbed with life and moving throngs. Unhitched vehicles stood in a tangled maze among the trees. And the whole took on the aspect of a huge carnival, pausing for a brief, pulsing interlude in its trek through the wilderness.

Ollie had gone to the church much later than usual that night. The sky remained clear and brilliant, although the moon had begun to wane. A light breeze played in the branches among the trees, and the crowd, as it swarmed and frolicked below, seemed strangely silent and listless now. Only laughter and loud talk rang sharp and crystal-clear against the drift of the wind.

Slaughter, Shell and Willie were standing in front of the church by the road when Ollie walked up, and both Slaughter and Willie caught her by the arm and escorted her to Alex's stand, and proceeded to vie with each other to buy her food and drink. But Ollie only took a sandwich and a glass of lemonade, and both men took nickels from their pockets and laid them on the counter.

So they stood there in the crowd, the two men talking in low tones, while the girl ate the sandwich and sipped lemonade. Shell had remained where he stood by the road in front of the church, and some moments later the other two had rejoined him there, their faces more sorrowful than before. But, now, they stood there talking to Ollie and watching that vague, distant look about her face and eyes. That look had been there the night before, when Willie came up on her down by the sweetgum, and it lingered about her eyes now, im-

184

parting to them the slow tension of still agony.

Willie was saying, "Guess you is feelin' good an' rested now, Mis' Ollie. Guess us kin walk around some, lak whut us was talkin' 'bout las' night." He grinned and glanced at Slaughter, but the girl didn't say anything.

Then Slaughter said, "Ef you don't feels lak walkin' none right now, Mis' Ollie, us could go out yonder an' set in Cap Downer's buggy. Cap done sey dat I kin use his buggy ef I wants to."

"She don't feel lak settin' in no buggy," Willie said, "wid all de peoples walkin' around an' habin' dey fun—does you, Mis' Ollie?"

The girl stood there, and still she didn't say anything. Just sipped her drink, glancing first at Slaughter and then at Willie, an odd empty smile touching her lips. Then she shook her head slowly, as though in answer to a question that hadn't been asked; and Slaughter said, leaning suddenly forward, "Would you lak to set out dere in de buggy a while sho nuff, Mis' Ollie?"

The girl emptied the glass and took a step forward and placed it on the counter. Then she turned and spoke for the first time. She said, "Hit's nice fer you all to treat me like dis. Only I ain't hongry or nuthin'." She paused, breathing deeply. "Guess I'll be goin' now," she went on, her eyes drifting away. "I thanks you all jes de same."

She turned to move away, and Willie said suddenly, "Mind ef I go 'long, Mis' Ollie? Jes—jes to sort of keep you comp'ny?"

"Some other time I wouldn't mind, Willie," she said, turning slowly around again. "But jes now I wants to walk by myse'f—see ef I kin see anybody dat I knows—anybody from down where I used to live."

She stood there an instant longer, watching their solemn, wet faces. Then she said again, "I thanks you all jes de same," and disappeared through the crowd.

She went down through the grove, picking her way slowly between the wagons and buggies. Mules and horses stood about in thick clusters, biting corn from the cob and nibbling at bundles of fodder, their rumps turned back to back. Here and there violent kicking sprees broke out among the animals and their owners came running. Then the kicking died down and peace was restored, and the girl kept picking up her feet and stepping over wagon tongues and going between buggies and around the trees. She made her way silently. The shadows were thick and deep. Here and there the moon broke through, and faces, etched sharply against the light, loomed into view and disappeared. She saw the road stretch white and silent beyond the blackness of the trees.

She emerged from the grove and stood in the road, the deep sand a white blaze before her eyes. She turned down the road toward the sweetgum tree, and her eyes kept watching a man standing there in almost the same spot she had stood the night before. He stood with his shoulder propped against the tree trunk, his back half turned. Then he straightened suddenly and looked around, and the girl stopped dead in her tracks. Her eyes blurred. She closed her eyes and a thin sweat broke out on her forehead. She caught at her lips with her teeth to keep them from trembling, and her body swayed back and forth on her feet, as though she were going to faint.

187

She said, "Jule!" and went quickly forward. The man stood there watching her coming toward him without moving.

She stopped in the shadow of the tree just short of the spot where the man stood. She said, "Jule! When you git here, Jule?" She reached out and caught hold of his hands, and her lips quivered and broke into a smile.

"Jes rode up a while ago," Jule said, watching her face and glancing around with a darting movement of his eyes. Then he released his hands and slipped them under her arms and down around her waist, and they stood there in the strained, hot silence, while mules brayed and the crowd frolicked in the churchyard. The braying of the mules sounded far off, against the drift of the wind, like a singing. . . .

When Jule finally released his arms, the girl stepped back and looked up at his face again. She could see his face plainly now, the leanness of it, with his eyes staring down at her, like sharply pointed lights. Her eyes held his an instant, then wavered and followed the lines of his neck to the junction of his throat and shoulders, where the blue

188

shirt and jumper opened at the collar. His shoulders seemed broader now than she had remembered them. They seemed to spread out from the base of his neck at angles almost like wings.

"You—you done come by yo'self, Jule?" she said then. "You—you didn't bring nobody wid you, did you?" Her eyes leaped back to his face.

"Yeh, I come by myse'f," Jule told her. "Rode my mule up." He continued to watch her face. He watched it with a cold sort of intensity, as though it fascinated him. Her eyes, the whites of them, glowed strangely.

"Den—den—you don't have to go back to Roba to-night, do you?" . . .

Jule looked away. "Speck I'll be ridin' back after de meetin'," he said slowly, and his voice sounded a little tired.

"Can't you stay tell to-morrow? Can't you ride back in de mornin', Jule?" The words quivered and tumbled from her lips, her breath catching. "You could—could stay tell to-morrow, couldn't you?" she went on, and her eyes blazed.

Jule was silent. He looked at her face again with

189

a sudden stab of his eyes, and said, "I sort of promised to be back after de meetin'—promised I wouldn't stay too long."

Ollie said, "Oh—," and caught her breath. She continued to look at his face, as though it were something she saw only from a distance—something she couldn't quite reach. His face kept drifting away and bouncing back before her eyes, like an image in a dream. She said irrelevantly, "You didn't stop by Della's on yo' way up, did you, Jule?"

There was an instant's silence.

"Della is dead," Jule said.

Ollie said, "Dead?" She whispered it.

"Dey buried her day befo'e yestiddy," Jule said.

Ollie stood without moving. The balls of her eyes stood up, like swollen bubbles, in their sockets. She said, "Della is—is dead, Jule?" and something in her face went suddenly cold—seemed to freeze there. Her lips began to tremble. She caught at her lips with her hands, stilled them.

"She died sometime Saddy night," Jule went on. "Dey found her dead. Didn't you hear 'bout hit?"

Ollie continued to stare at Jule's face and her face

began to sweat. She held out her hand and caught hold of Jule's arm. Then her body gave a little lurch and pitched against his huge bulk. Her arms went around his waist and her face buried itself against his breast. She cried, "Jule, Jule—oh, Jule! . . . Della ain't—ain't dead fer true, is she, Jule? She ain't real, real, cold dead, is she?"

Her arms tightened and her body trembled.

"Dey buried her day befo'e yestiddy," Jule repeated. "I rode to de buryin' on my mule." He lifted her face from his chest and looked at it, and Ollie stood up suddenly straight, her eyes glancing away.

She said slowly, "Della is—is dead, cold dead!" and looked at Jule again. "You—you done killed Della, Jule," she went on quietly, and watched a queer look flash across his face. "I—I don't means you killed her wid yo' hands or nuthin' like dat," she amended quickly. "I—I means Della couldn't live widout you, Jule. She wanted you. Wanted you jes—jes like I wanted you. Only—" Her breathing went hissing through her teeth. "Only she couldn't want you an'—an' keep on livin' an' not

191

hab you, like I could. . . . I guess Della was gittin'
ol'. I guess she wa'n't young no mo' like me an' dis
new 'oman you is got now. I guess she was jes
natchl'y weak fer you—so weak dat . . ."

Her voice trailed off and her eyes were a little
wet. Jule watched her eyes, could see the water
spilling from them and rolling over her cheek bones
and dripping to the ground.

He sighed, shifting awkwardly in his tracks, and
said, "I don't guess hit was nuthin' lak dat, Ollie."

"I knows, Jule," Ollie said simply. " 'Cause I done
talked wid Della—done live wid her! Done live
thru de same thing she done had to live thru." She
dropped her head and stood silent for a moment.
Then she looked up suddenly, and said: "You—you
wants to go by home wid me fer a while? You
could go on back to Roba from down dere, ef you
want to."

Jule stood quite still, without speaking, his eyes
watching her. Then he caught at her body with his
arms and crushed it.

He said, "You wants to go now? You don't
wants to stay to de meetin'?"

Ollie shook her head, and her lips said, "Yeh—
yeh—I wants to go now! . . . Us could have longer
to stay an' talk, ef—ef us goes now!" She wasn't
looking at his face now, but beyond it, where the
couples walked silently in the road and disappeared
over the hill toward the frog pond.

The singing had started when Jule came back
from the grove with his mule. He had hooked the
stirrups over the saddle horn, and he and Ollie
circled the grove and headed down the road toward
Alex's, leading the mule. They walked side by side
in the middle of the road, and Ollie told him about
the last time she had seen Della. She didn't say
anything about the night she had sat in his cabin,
waiting for him to come home. She spoke of the
days and nights she had spent with Della, and of
the things that Della had told her concerning the
new girl he had at Roba yonder.

"Della sey dat she is kind o' pretty-lookin'," Ollie
pointed out, "an' dat you all is fixin' to git married."

"I don't guess nuthin' lak dat gwine happen,"
Jule told her. "We jes sort of met up an' started to

193

goin' 'round toget'er after you tuck an' went off lak you did."

"I thought you jes wanted to be wid Della," Ollie said, "after she done give you dat cabin to stay in."

"I ain't nevah jes wanted to be wid Della," Jule said.

"But you left an' went up dere when she give you dat house," Ollie reminded him. "You left an' sey dat—dat I could come along ef I wanted to."

"Dat don't sey dat I jes wanted to be wid Della," Jule repeated.

"But you done went jes de same, didn't you? You done left me yonder at de Crossroads, didn't you?"

"I jes went 'cause she kept on after me," Jule said. "I figgered dat ef I goes on up dere an' stay a while, an' she sees dat I ain't got no real feelin' fer her—I figgered dat she'd leave me 'lone."

"You didn't eben make up yo' mind to love her a li'l bit?" Ollie said, glancing sideways at his face.

"In a way, I ain't make up my mind to love no-body," Jule said.

The girl was silent. She watched the road as they went up a slope by the schoolhouse and headed

194

down another slope. The road looked queer and white and flat. The fields and hedging thickets looked queer and white, too, with the paleness of the moon upon them. Then low clouds began floating across the sky, shading the moon, and the fields and thickets grew dark and only the road remained white with the sand.

"You means," the girl said then, "you ain't nevah make up yo' mind to love nobody?"

"I sey in a way, I ain't," Jule said, and once again Ollie was silent.

Then she said, "Den—den you don't love dis 'oman you is stayin' wid now? I means, you don't hab no real deep-down feelin' fer her or nuthin'?"

"No; in a way I don't," Jule said.

"You means—not de kind o' feelin' dat'd make you want to marry her, is dat it?"

"Yeh," Jule said. "Dat's whut you want me to sey anyway, ain't hit?" He glanced at her face.

Ollie didn't answer. She said, "Is you—you evah had de kind o' feelin' dat's make you want to marry me, Jule?"

But Jule didn't answer either. So they walked on

195

down the road until they came to the thicket just below Knute's and Bell's shack, and Ollie paused suddenly, and said: "I guess we bettah leave de mule in here somewhere, so nobody won't see her standin' around when dey be comin' from de meetin'."

"All right," Jule said.

They turned off to the right and entered the thicket and followed the banks of a stream between the trees.

It was dark walking beneath the trees now. Clouds were getting thicker and the moon was dimmed. Jule said, "Speck hit's gwine rain befo'e mornin'." But Ollie remained silent. They walked on, passing the spot where she and Willie had come that morning from old Lucy's party, until they came to a circular opening among the trees.

Ollie stopped and glanced around. She said, "Guess dis is all right, huh, Jule?"

"Yeh," Jule said, and unstrapped the saddle and pulled it from the mule's back, while Ollie made a halter with one end of the rope and fitted it about the animal's face underneath the bridle. Then she slipped the bit from the animal's mouth and Jule

196

tied the other end of the rope to a swinging branch, leaving enough slack for the mule to wallow. Then they went up a steep incline and out into the open.

The fields were darker now. Trees and distant houses seemed to squat and clutch at the earth and the air was still. Only floating clouds seemed restless, with the moon racing and dipping through from behind them, and then hiding its face again, like a peeping child.

"Speck hit's gwine rain sho' nuff," Jule said, glancing up at the clouds. But Ollie kept her eyes leveled on a straight line in front of her. They seemed to be staring at something in the distance they couldn't quite see. Staring and thinking. Her eyes were glassy—kind of clean and fresh-looking.

Jule caught her arm and they went down a sharp descent, crossed the road, and climbed through the gap in the rail fence. Then they followed a trail that led across a picked cotton-field to Ollie's cabin.

Ollie lit a torch and Jule pulled off his jumper and sat down in a chair, his eyes wandering about the room. The room was spotlessly clean. He sat there gazing at the floor and the walls and the rafters

197

overhead, while the girl went back to the bed and pulled off her shoes and stockings. Then Ollie walked back across the floor in her bare feet and stood there beside Jule, in front of the fireplace, looking down at the fire. Then she turned and sat down across his lap and tucked the hem of her dress about her knees.

She said, "You wants me to fix you some victuals to eat, Jule?"

"I ain't hongry," Jule said.

"Only take a minute to fry a egg an' warm ovah some bread I got here," Ollie said.

"Don't feel lak eatin' nuthin' now," Jule said.

"Den I'll fix somethin' fer you befo'e you go," Ollie said. "You might be kind o' hongry-like den."

"Don't aim to stay dat long. Jes goin' to stay a li'l while."

"But hit's early yet, Jule!"

She twisted her body around in his lap, so that her face lay flat on one side against his chest.

"De meetin' ain't out tell after midnight," Ollie went on, slipping her arms underneath his and extending them around his ribs to the dent in his back.

198

"An' you could stay tell after den—tell after de peoples done come back from de church." Her fingers touched, twisted themselves together in a kind of knot, and were still.

The torch burned slowly down and Jule was silent. The coals turned red in the ashes and the room grew dark with the rich red of the coals. But Ollie didn't stir to replenish the blaze. She merely sat there on Jule's lap and watched the room grow dim about her with the dying embers.

Then her body relaxed a little. Jule sat up straight, supporting her body. The coals popped, turned gray one by one, then black.

Ollie said, "I feels kind o' sleepy now." And there was silence. She said, "You feels sleepy too, Jule?" Jule didn't answer. She said, "Hit'd be nice to go to sleep now, wouldn't it, Jule? . . ."

The floor did creak a little when Jule got to his feet with the girl in his arms. The room was black and silent now.

CHAPTER XVI

It was raining and Jule was snoring. People kept passing along the road, coming from church, talking in the rain. Their voices sounded flat and loud, for the rain was thin. Ollie listened to the rain. But voices and thudding hoofs and clucking wagons kept coming in an endless stream and going down the road. She listened to hear Alex's wagon go by, with Nan's loud talk and Knute's heavy laughter. But she didn't hear Alex's wagon. They all sounded alike: clucking wheels, plodding hoofs, and loud country talk. Then the wagons began to thin out and go by one at a time; then ceased altogether. And there was only the sound of Jule's heavy breathing and the rain slanting against the roof. The rain fell in thin, nervous sheets, and huge drops of it seeped through between the boards and dripped into puddles there on the floor.

Ollie didn't move. She lay there, listening, her

body flattened against the mattress. Her body used to feel things—used to live and breathe and respond to things. But now it only felt a little numb. She ran her fingers along the surface of her thighs to her knees and wondered what her thighs felt like. But neither her thighs nor her fingers had any feelings now. They were just parts of her body and her body felt peacefully dead! She could get up and leave her body there beside Jule until it ached and came alive again, if she wanted to. Then she could come back to it and repossess it, and Jule could go on back to Roba yonder.

Jule wouldn't bother her body. He'd forget even to notice that it was there. He'd just get up and put on his clothes and slip out through the door and across the field and saddle his mule. Then he'd swing up in the saddle, set his spurs against the mule's flanks, and ride through the dawn to Roba in the rain. And her body would still be there. And she'd get it and put on her clothes and go on up to the yard and help Nan and Mae Jane with the milking. She'd milk two cows to their one and balance one pail of the milk on her head, letting the other two swing from her wrists, and go swiftly up the trail to the house, her feet tripping lightly through the dawn.

Caroline would watch her coming up the kitchen steps and laugh out loud. "Gal," Caroline would say, "you is feelin' right frisky dis mornin', ain't you, honey?" And Ollie would say, "No'm; I jes wanted to git thru wid de milkin' as quick as I could on account of de rain. Dat's all, Mis' Ca'line." And Caroline would grin and look at her eyes, and say, "Now, gal, you knows you is feelin' sort o' frisky dis mornin'! Look at dem eyes o' your'n! . . . Lordy, honey, I speck ef I didn't knowed you was stayin' yonder in dat shack by yo'self—I speck I'd 'clare befo'e de Lord dat you is been friskin' around somewhere you ain't got no business." Caroline would laugh again, and add: "I speck I would now sho' nuff, honey!"

Ollie would giggle and settle the pails on the table and begin pouring the milk through the strainer into the churn. Then Nan and Mae Jane would come up the steps into the kitchen with one pail each, and Nan would start her mouth to running.

"Look heah, gal!" Nan would say. "What's done git into you? Don't you knows dat you can't be pullin' an' jerkin' on dem cows' tits lak you was dis mornin'? . . . You ain't done gone plumb crazy or nuthin', is you?"

"No'm, I ain't done gone crazy, Mis' Nan," Ollie would say. "I was jes—jes tryin' to do a li'l more, so you all wouldn't hab to do so much on account of hit rainin', I guess."

"Hit's been rainin' befo'e dis an' you ain't nevah done dat much, is you?"

Nan's eyes would snap, but Ollie wouldn't say any more. She'd sit down to the table and begin eating her breakfast, and Caroline would say gently, "Leave de gal 'lone now, Nan. She jes felt lak doin' more'n her part to sort o' help out dis mornin'. Dat's all." And Ollie would go on eating. She'd eat up everything Caroline put before her, and Caroline would look at the empty plates—then at the girl—and shake her head despairingly.

"Lordy, honey," Caroline would moan, "I don't know whut's done happened to you sho' nuff! Alex can't go on feedin' no gal whut kin eat lak dis! . . ."

204

Daylight and it was still raining. Jule was gone. Ollie sat up suddenly straight and stared around the room. Then she dropped back on her pillow and looked up at the roof. The rain sounded dull and listless now, and the wind was blowing up cold. Ollie said aloud, "Jule done gone an' hit's still rainin' . . . an' he nevah even woke me up to sey good-by when he was leavin'!" She turned wearily on her side and watched the gray dawn creep through the cracks between the logs.

She lay there staring at the logs and listening to the rain. Then there was a sudden thrust against the door, and Jule squatted through the door into the room, with the wet saddle on his back.

Ollie stiffened and sat up again. She said, "Jule!" —and a flicker of a smile touched her lips. "I thought you done gone to Roba, Jule. I thought you done forgot to sey—"

"De saddle done got wet," Jule said, and heaved the wet leather in the corner behind the door. He turned and faced the girl, water dripping from his sleeves and wetting the floor.

"Den you is gwine stay tell de rain clears up?" Ollie's face brightened.

"Got to stay, I guess," Jule said. "Only I ain't got no feed or nuthin' fer my mule."

"I kin git some feed fer yo' mule," Ollie said. "I kin fetch some back from de lot yonder, when I goes to milk de cows." She reached for her dress lying there across the foot of the bed and pulled it on quickly over her head, and drew it down snugly around her waist and hips. It was the same dress she had worn to the meeting the night before—starched gingham, with a pleated blouse, and crisply ironed.

"I guess I ought to hab gone on back las' night lak I started," Jule said, moving toward the fireplace.

"But you kin stay here, Jule!" the girl said. "You kin stay here 'long as you want to. I guess I is kind o' glad hit's rainin' like hit is so—so you kin stay."

She swung her feet over the side of the bed and slipped them into a pair of old shoes there on the floor. Then she stood up and looked at Jule stand-

206

ing there before the fireplace, gazing down at the dead ashes.

"All de same, I guess I should hab gone on back," Jule said. "I guess—"

"But you kin stay here wid me, can't you?" Ollie said. "You don't jes hab to go back to Roba less'n you want to, do you?"

Jule turned slowly around. He said, "Whut you mean, I don't jes hab to go back less'n I want to?"

"I means—dis other 'oman don't means dat much to you, dat you is jes got to go back, do she?"

"Hit ain't what she means," Jule said, and Ollie was silent.

She watched his face, tying the bow at the back of her dress and moving toward the fireplace. Then she said, "But you wa'n't like dat when me an' you was stayin' toget'er, Jule. You didn't mind goin' off an' stayin'—"

"Maybe I didn't," Jule said. "But dis is different."

He sank down in a chair and rubbed his wet hands together and looked at the ashes. And Ollie said, "Oh, I see," and dropped to her knees and began building a fire mechanically with her fingers.

207

Moments passed. Then Ollie said, "Us don't hab to quarrel none whilst you is here, do us, Jule? You kin stay 'long as you want to an' go when you git ready, but us don't hab to fuss an' carry on, do us?"

Jule said, "Nuh; us don't hab to fuss," and held out his hands to the blazing fire. " 'Tain't no need fer me an' you to start fussin' now, I don't guess." He rubbed his hands again and looked at the fire.

Ollie stood up then, and said, "You stay here by the fire an' dry yo' clothes, an' ef you wants to you kin go back to bed an' git some sleep. I'll fetch somethin' back fer you an' de mule both to eat."

She went back to the head of the bed and took down her jumper and buttoned it snugly about her throat. Then she pulled on a cap and went through the door out into the rain. And Jule sat there in front of the fire.

Ollie brought back hard corn in a sack for the mule, and eggs and butter and molasses on a plate for Jule. She made coffee in a skillet over the fire and warmed over some bread. And while Jule ate, she shucked the corn in her wood-box and covered it

208

over with the sack and took it to the mule. She watered the animal at the branch and tied her up again before returning to the house. And it was good daylight when she finished these chores, the rain coming down in a steady pour.

Ollie had told Willie to give her the corn in a sack, when she went past the crib door on her way to milk the cows. "Whut you gwine do wid corn in a sack, Mis' Ollie?" Willie had said.

"Jes put hit in a sack an' hide de sack under de crib," Ollie had told him. " 'Bout twelve or fo'teen ears." And this the boy had done.

When Ollie went to the house with her milk, Caroline said, "Gal, whut you wearin' dat good dress 'round heah in de rain fer?"

"I jes put hit on, Mis' Caroline," Ollie said, "jes 'cause hit was rainin' an' dere ain't gwine be no work in de field."

"But dat's one o' yo' good dresses, ain't hit?"

"Yes'm; but hit needs washin' already, Mis' Ca'-line."

Caroline looked at the girl sharply. Then she said, "Well, where was you las' night at de meetin', honey? De rain done come up an' Alex done had evahbody at de church lookin' fer you so you could ride back in de wagon wid us."

"I done come on home befo'e de rain started," Ollie said. "I sort of figgered dat hit was gwine rain, so I come on home."

"But dat ain't lak you to come on home," Caroline said, "de way you laks to hab a good time."

"Maybe hit ain't," Ollie said, and giggled softly. "But dat was de way I figgered las' night." She poured her milk through the strainer into the churn. Then she said, "I wants to take my victuals back to de cabin yonder, 'cause I ain't so hongry right now, Mis' Ca'line."

"Take yo' victuals to de cabin in de rain?"

"Yes'm."

Caroline said, "Lord hab mussy, Jesus! You young niggers gwine run all de ol' peoples clean outa dey senses! You wants to do dis an' den you wants to do dat—an' hit ain't no tellin' whut you gwine want to do next! . . . Gal, I don't care where you take yo' victuals, jes since you fetch dat plate back."

Caroline sighed and shook her head, her lips

breaking into a knowing grin. "Go on an' take yo' victuals to yo' cabin, honey," she said.

So Ollie had taken her breakfast to Jule. . . .

Jule had finished eating when Ollie returned from feeding the mule. His jumper hung on the back of the chair. He had slipped his feet out of his shoes and unbuttoned his shirt at the throat, and his clothes were practically dry now.

"Did you hab enough to eat, Jule?" Ollie said, stripping the jumper from her back and hanging it on a nail behind the bed.

"Yeh," Jule said. "Left some fer you."

"But I didn't mean fer you to leave me none, Jule."

"You ain't eat already, is you?"

"I wa'n't really hongry, Jule. I—I brought dat fer you." She stood there before the fire, looking down at Jule's face.

"How you done eat an' fetch dis here, too?" Jule said.

The girl was silent. Then she said, "But I didn't mean fer you to leave me none, Jule! I—"

"Come on an' eat," Jule said. "I done had enough." He stood up and stretched. "Guess I'll lay down a while. I feels kind o' sleepy."

He went back to the bed and began pulling off his clothes, and Ollie sat down in his chair and ate what was left in the plate. Then she stood up and put more wood on the fire and went back to the bed where Jule was. . . .

The rain continued all day and all that night and broke the next morning. The sun rose, vivid and clear, and the fields were bright and wet with the dampness of the rain. Jule had gone out of the door at daylight, with the saddle draped across his back. Ollie had stood there watching after him, as he went up the trail across the cotton field and disappeared through the gap into the road. She had stood there gazing at the trail over which Jule had gone, the dawn getting brighter and brighter about her, her eyes staring. Jule hadn't said when he was coming back, and Ollie hadn't asked. He had said, "Well, I guess I'll be goin', Ollie. So long!" And he had picked up the saddle.

"So long, Jule," Ollie had said. "Guess you won't

*He Went Back to Bed and Began Pull-
ing Off His Clothes, and Ollie Sat
Down in His Chair and Ate What
Was Left in the Plate.*

come back to de meetin' to-night, will you? Hit's de las' night!"

"I don't guess so," Jule had said. And that had been all. He didn't speak of the girl at Roba or anything, and neither did Ollie. He just picked up the saddle and went out the door and up the trail and disappeared.

The last night of the meeting was in full swing when Ollie arrived at the church. The grounds had had a chance to dry and the rain didn't affect the size of the crowd. People were there from Hurtsboro and Little Texas and Fort Davis, and Sandy Kennebrew had parked his buggy out by the sweetgum tree, with demijohns of corn whiskey hid under the seat. The crowd was jolly, but their eyes seemed a little sad. Fights had been scarce, and there hadn't been a cutting scrape during the meeting.

"Hit don't look lak dem ol'-timey meetin's us used to hab," some of the older heads kept saying. "Nuh, hit don't," some of the others said. "Dis young crowd ain't wild lak dey used to be. Dey used to ride dey mules up from de swamp an' Hannon, wid

215

pistols an' razors an' evahthing—lookin' fer trouble!
. . . Dey used to be comin' up de road an' thru de
swamp, ridin' an' whoopin' jes as loud as dey could,
wid dey pistols poppin' lak dey was gwine to war!
. . . You could hear dem mules' hoofs fer miles,
comin' down de road jes as fas' as dey could come,
an' mighty nigh evah night dere was some cuttin'
an' some shootin', too!"

"Nuh," the older heads kept saying, "hit ain't lak
dem ol'-timey meetin's us used to hab. . . ."

Ollie had stopped at the well to get a drink of
water. (The road was getting dry and dusty again.)
Then she stood around a while and watched the
crowd. People kept driving up in buggies and
wagons and going into the grove in search of a
hitching post for their mules. People with strange,
shiny faces she had never seen before. They kept
passing and calling out greetings to those already on
the grounds, their voices ringing quick and loud.

"Howdy, Sis Martha!" . . . "Howdy, Babe! Lordy,
gal, I ain't seed you since de las' camp meetin'! How
you done come 'way down heah?" . . . "Peoples,
yonder is Cousin Callie! Lemma speak to ol' Cuz!

216

Howdy, Cuz!" . . . "Howdy yo'self, Cuz! How you is?" . . . "Lordy, ol' Cuz done come all de way from 'bove Magnolia yonder. . . ."

Ollie stood there listening, her eyes staring, as though she wondered why all the people were there. People, people, people—and more people! She kept watching them—listening to them—and they kept driving up in wagons and going into the grove. And there on the grounds around the stands, they kept marching to and fro, up to the church and back down the lane, like queer creatures whose faces and bodies might've been shells, and whose voice had become now the clatter of sounding brass. They kept marching and Ollie went on watching. She stared as though a barrier had been raised between her and them—as though they existed in another world apart from her, and she was no longer one among them. . . . As though, for her, the meeting had ended two nights ago. For Jule had come and gone!

"Jule! . . ."

The word slipped from her lips and she turned her head and looked down the lane. People were rushing down that way now. Running in droves, their voices strained with excitement. A crowd was forming a circle at the foot of the lane, just above the sweetgum tree in the middle of the big road, and it stood there in the moonlight, thick and soundless, watching.

Ollie hurried down the lane and circled the crowd until she came to a spot where the people weren't so thick. Then she began working her way between standing bodies, side-stepping children and smaller folk, and leaping over bent, peeping forms. And here and there whispers ran through the crowd: "Is de gal got a razor?" . . . "She ain't fixin' to cut de man, is she?" . . . "Lordy, is you evah seed sich a mess as dis!"

As Ollie reached the center of the group, the crowd surged backwards, and she saw Jule standing there in the clearing, the moon as bright as liquid against his face. Ollie paused, her eyes taking in all that lay before her. The girl, facing Jule there, was a slight thing. Her face, in the moonlight, wore the simple dignity of a madonna, and she kept taking a step forward, her right hand concealed beneath the folds of her skirt, her eyes leveled on Jule.

218

Her voice was low-pitched. She spit her words through her teeth with a kind of rattle. She kept saying, "All I wants to know is where you been since night befo'e las'? . . . You sey you was comin' here to dis meetin'. You sey you ain't gwine nowhere else but to dis meetin'. You sey you was comin' back soon as de meetin' was ovah. An' den, den—God damn you!—you stay away las' night an' de night befo'e, an' I got out dis mornin' an' walked all de way up here, lookin'—"

Ollie had stepped forward into the clearing then, and a queer hissing went rippling through the crowd. Jule said something and caught at Ollie's shoulder, swinging her around and away. But Ollie twisted free of his grasp and faced the girl again. She said, "He stayed wid me, miss." She said it so calmly that the other stood there an instant, her eyes staring, as if stunned. Then her eyes blazed slowly, like fanned sparks, and she said, "An' jes who might you be?"

"Dey calls me Ollie Miss," Ollie said simply, "ef dat means anything to you."

The other girl's reply was simple. Her right arm

219

swung out and around, and the crowd stood as if frozen in its tracks. Jule's hand got a second grip on Ollie's shoulder at almost the same instant the razor struck. And the razor, instead of hitting Ollie's neck, slid down from her shoulder and across her ribs and went under her arm and around to the small part of her back. . . .

When Alex reached the scene, Jule had Ollie up in his arms, turning around in circles, as though he didn't know where to go or what to do. Two men had caught the other girl from behind, twisting her arm until she dropped the razor. Women were screaming. Some had fainted. And people kept running away from the scene and back to it again, like animals in a stampede.

Alex could see the blood. It was dripping from Jule's wrist and arm about Ollie's waist and making dark blotches there in the sand. The upper part of her dress was soaked.

Alex made Jule place the girl on the ground again, flat on her back, and he cut the clothing from the upper part of her body and laid the wound bare.

Somebody spread a quilt on the ground then, and Alex shifted her to this to keep grit out of the wound. Some of the men went running to the well for water. Others went to the stands for sugar; and "Stump-tail" Wiley went to the church and fetched a hatful of soot and cobwebs from the church stove.

Alex didn't use the water and the sugar. He worked with the soot and cobwebs, dressing the wound from the front and working around under her arm to her back, while Uncle Len and old Hamp held the crowd back with shot guns under their arms. The moon was bright, but lanterns were brought and placed in a circle there on the ground around Alex and the girl.

Alex worked alone, silently, swiftly. And people stood there watching him smear the soot into the wound, their wet faces staring. Now and then a woman caught her breath deeply, with the simple utterance: "Lawd hab mussy, Jesus." Then there was silence again.

When the blood ceased to flow, Alex stood up, and the crowd drew nearer and began to peep. Ollie didn't move. She lay there, flat on her back, her eyes half closed. People began to whisper, "Reckon she dead?" But there was no answer, and they went on staring with shiny, fixed faces.

Alex turned and saw Slaughter, Shell and Willie standing there in a group. He beckoned to Slaughter and told him to borrow a mule and go to Hurtsboro as fast as he could for a doctor. Then he told Shell and Willie to get the mules in harness and drive the wagon around there.

When the wagon came, somebody had placed a mattress in the bottom of it. Alex and three other men picked Ollie up on the quilt and laid her on the mattress, and the wagon turned and drove off down the road. Then Alex turned and began searching around. But Jule and the other girl had disappeared. Only the blood and the razor remained there in the sand where Ollie had fallen.

Alex and Three Other Men Picked Ol-
lie Up on the Quilt and Laid Her On
the Mattress, and the Wagon Turned
and Drove Off Down the Road.

CHAPTER XVII

It was long past midnight when the doctor arrived. The cotton field surrounding Ollie's cabin resembled the camp meeting in the churchyard, with groups of waiting people. Only there weren't any stands where they could buy things. Some were sitting on the bare ground about the cabin. Others were perched on their mules or were sitting on the rail fence out by the road, whispering in low tones and looking up at the moon. And still others stood about in huddles, sighing and talking and staring off into the night. Again and again, somebody would say, "Reckon she gwine die?" But there was no answer, save—"I don't see how nobody kin git cut lak dat an' keep on livin'."

Then another would say, "I hopes she don't die. I don't laks to see nobody die 'bout nuthin'."

"Can't help dat," still another would say. "When you is got to die, you is got to die, an' hit don't make no difference ef hit's 'bout somethin' or nuthin'."

Silence. Then, "Well, whut dis gal done cut Ollie 'bout anyhow?"

" 'Bout a man," was the answer. "Hit's always 'bout a man when one 'oman cut another 'oman."

"Was de man dere?"

"Course he was dere. Didn't you see him? Him an' dis other 'oman was cussin' an' carryin' on at one another when Ollie walked up."

"Well, how come Ollie done git messed up in hit, ef de cussin' was betwix dem two?"

"Lawd only knows," was the answer. "Less'n dis man was Ollie's man, too. Dat's de way de 'omans an' de mens is dese days."

Silence again, until Caroline or some of the others came out of the cabin to go to the yard to get something for the doctor. Then they'd gather around Caroline and begin asking questions. But Caroline wouldn't answer any questions. She'd keep on walking and say, "You niggers git on you all's mules an' go on home. De gal ain't fixin' to die yet."

"Us jes wants to know ef de doctor gwine sew her up—dat's all, Mis' Ca'line?" one of them would say.

226

"Shut up, fool!" Caroline would say. "Course de doctor gwine sew her up!"

They'd go back to their places then, where they had been sitting or standing, and Caroline would go on up to the yard. The whispering would continue, the air getting cooler with the settling dew, the moon sinking lower and lower toward the west. An owl hooted somewhere in the distance. Night birds trilled their weird, musical notes. And still they waited, staring off into the night and listening.

Day was breaking when the doctor left the cabin with his satchel, and tiny groups about the cabin got to their feet. They stood silently, watching the doctor, as he went up the trail to the fence and climbed into his buggy there in the road. Then they gathered and stood in front of the cabin door—staring at the door—and waited.

It was quite a while before Alex came to the door and said that Ollie was sleeping and there was nothing more any one could do just now.

"Den she ain't gwine die, is she, Un' Alex?" one of them said.

"She's sleepin'," Alex repeated. "Doctor say she got to git some sleep."

"How many stitches de doctor done took?" another said then.

"Stitches don't matter," Alex said. "You all just go on home. Ain't no more us kin do now."

Some of them departed, but most of them continued to wait. They stood there looking up at Alex —watching his face—as though they wanted to say something more, but weren't sure just what that something was. So they just stood there and stared. And Alex tilted his body to one side there in the doorway, waiting and looking down on them, his eyes deeply set in their sockets. His eyes seemed heavy and a little tired now.

Caroline came to the door and stood there beside Alex. Then Nan and Mae Jane came. All of their eyes looked tired except Nan's. Nan's eyes were bright and kind of fresh-looking. They glittered like cat's eyes.

Caroline said, "Why don't you all go on home? Alex done told you de gal is sleepin'!"

"We jes—jes—" one of them began. Then they

228

all turned and began moving away, as though their actions were the efforts of a single person. Then they paused again, a few yards from the cabin, and looked back at Alex and the women.

Nan squeezed through the door and went up the trail, as though she were going home. Alex and Caroline stepped back in the cabin and glanced at the girl lying there on the bed. The girl was breathing evenly. So they came out again and pulled the door shut behind them. . . .

The rays of the sun were slanting across the fields when the last of the crowd departed. And they knew all about the stitches! Nan had told them when Alex stepped inside the cabin with Caroline to look at Ollie. "Hit was forty!" Nan had whispered. "I counted evah las' one of dem!"

"Forty stitches!" they echoed under their breaths, and went on home. . . .

Alex and Caroline went on to the yard, and Nan and Mae Jane followed them a pace or two to the rear. Shell, Slaughter and Willie took seats there on Ollie's steps. They'd wait there until one of the women had finished her morning's chores and would be free to stay with Ollie.

They sat there a while without speaking, looking at the ground, the dewy grass giving off a fresh clean smell.

Then Slaughter said, "I ain't dreamt nuthin' lak dis was gwine happen." He said it quietly, his elbows resting on his knees.

"I knowed sump'n lak dis was bound to pop up," Shell said, and Willie was silent.

"I jes don't see how anybody could do sump'n lak dis to Mis' Ollie," Slaughter went on. "I ain't nevah seen her do nobody wrong."

"Well, somebody done done hit," Shell said. "So she musta done sump'n she ain't got no business doin'."

"All de same, I don't see hit." Slaughter sighed.

"Dat's because you is blind an' can't see nothin' nohow," Shell said. "An' den, maybe, you see hit an' don't want to see hit. Maybe dat feelin' you is got inside o' you fer her is makin' you blind."

Slaughter was silent, and still Willie didn't say anything.

230

Shell stood up and stretched. "Y'all two kin stay dere an' wait tell Nan or Mae Jane come back from milkin' de cows, ef you wants to. I gwine git some sleep. Uncle Alex mought want to finish pullin' dat corn a'ter dinner."

He walked off up the trail and Slaughter and Willie remained seated there on the steps. Slaughter didn't say any more, and Willie didn't break his silence. They simply sat there staring at the ground, or gazing off into the bright morning's sun, as though, in some strange way, they shared a kindred feeling.

Mae Jane came back to stay with Ollie, and the two men got up and went on to their room. They walked one behind the other up the narrow trail, their heads hanging, with Slaughter in the lead. And neither of them spoke.

Mae Jane sat there in the cabin and dozed while the girl slept. Now and then she'd awaken and glance around the room, then fall asleep again. The cabin was bright and still.

It was afternoon when Caroline came with food on a plate and hot coffee. The girl was still sleeping.

231

Caroline glanced at the bed and tiptoed across the floor to the fireplace where Mae Jane was sitting. She set the plate and cup on the hearth and started a blaze in the fireplace to keep them warm. Then she turned to Mae Jane and whispered, "She ain't woke up yet, is she?"

Mae Jane blinked her eyes open, and said, "Nuh— nuh—she ain't woke up. I ain't eben hear her move since I been settin' here."

"De doctor musta give her sump'n to make her sleep," Caroline said.

"I speck he did," Mae Jane said. "You know he given her dem white pills to take when he was leavin'." She was wide awake now.

"Yeh; I know," Caroline said.

There was silence. Caroline glanced about the room, her eyes taking in the walls, the bed, and the table there in the corner with the water bucket on it. The sun streamed through cracks in the roof and made checkered blocks of light there on the floor.

"You know she do keep dis cabin sort o' clean," Caroline said then.

"Yeh, she do," Mae Jane said. "An' hit's a pity she done git cut up lak dis, an' her bein' so clean an' nice lak she is."

"Hit sho' is a pity all right," Caroline said, and sighed.

Then Mae Jane said, "Ain't nobody knowed who dis gal was dat cut her, an' whut she done cut her 'bout?"

"Nobody ain't knowed yet," Caroline said. "Alex done sey he gwine send fer de sheriff soon as she git strong enough to talk an' tell whut led up to de cuttin'. You know de doctor sey she too weak now. She done lost too much blood. He sey—"

Ollie twisted a little in the bed then and groaned, and the two women were silent. They looked at each other and then at the bed. The girl became still again.

"Dat cut must be painin' her," Caroline said.

"Yeh, I guess so," Mae Jane said. "Dat 'oman musta been tryin' to cut de heart out o' her bosom to cut her lak dat."

"Hit sho' looks dat way all right," Caroline said, and there was silence again. She stood up straight

233

and looked at Mae Jane. "I guess you kin go on home an' git some sleep," she said then. "I kin set here an watch her a while."

"I ain't so sleepy now," Mae Jane said. "I kin stay a while longer an' you kin go back to de yard yonder. Dem boys ain't had dey victuals yet, is dey?"

"Dat's all right 'bout dey victuals," Caroline said. "Hits already cooked an' Alex kin sho'm where 'tis ef dey gits hongry. You go on home, 'cause somebody got to stay here both night an' day tell she git strong enough to stay by herse'f."

"All right den," Mae Jane said. "I'll go an' come back." She got to her feet and tiptoed across the floor, and Caroline sat down in the chair and placed another piece of kindling on the fire.

Later that afternoon, Slaughter and Willie brought an armful of fresh kindling and placed it in the box there by the fireplace. Slaughter said, "Uncle Alex done told us to chop dis up an' fetch hit down here, Mis' Ca'line."

"All right," Caroline said. "I speck one o' you all

bettah take dat bucket back an' fetch some fresh water, too."

"Yes'm, we'll fetch some," Slaughter said.

He reached for the bucket, but Willie had already picked it up. So they tiptoed back across the floor, glancing at the bed where the girl lay. Her eyes were closed and her face looked dry and ashen. Slaughter stared at her face a moment, then followed Willie through the door out into the yard.

Willie brought the water back alone, and later, Knute Kelly and Bell stopped by to ask how Ollie was feeling. "She still sleepin'," Caroline told them. "She ain't woke up since de doctor left dis mornin'."

Then Nan came. Caroline was sitting before the fireplace, smoking her pipe and watching the fire, when Nan entered the door. The plate and cup were there on the hearth and the girl hadn't moved since Mae Jane left. Nan drew up a chair and sat down.

"Well, I reckon Alex done see whut I done told him was right," Nan said, and looked at the plate.

"Now, Nan," Caroline said, "don't start dat ag'in."

"Start nuthin'!" Nan said. "De fust time I lay eyes

235

on dat gal, I knowed she was gwine mean trouble.
Alex ain't had no business to let her stay here in de
fust place."

Caroline said, "Nan, you please hush now? De
doctor done sey us got to keep de gal quiet on account o' her bein' so weak!"

"Nuh, I ain't gwine hush," Nan said. "Y'all
wouldn't listen to me in de beginnin', but you gwine
listen to me now! . . . Dat 'oman whut done cut
dis gal ain't done cut her 'bout nuthin'—you heah
dat!"

Caroline lifted the pipe from her teeth and spit
through the fire against the soot-covered bricks. "Us
knows hit was 'bout sump'n, Nan," she said. "But
hit don't do no good to talk 'bout hit now."

"Hit would've done some good ef Alex done listen
to me in de fust place. He wouldn't hab dis mess on
his hands now!"

"Won't you please hush, Nan? Jes shut up an'
hush!"

"Ain't I done told you I ain't gwine hush?" Nan
said. "Las' summer when dat gal went prowlin', she
236

went to see dis same man dat 'oman done cut her
'bout! 'Side o' dat—"

"How you knows dat's where she went, Nan?"

"I know hit jes lak I knows us is settin' here
lookin' at dat fire! Dat gal went to see dis man,
I tell you, whoever he is, an' fer all us knows he
mought've been comin' here all along to see her
right here in dis cabin! . . . 'Side o' dat—"

"Peoples, will you listen to dis 'oman!" Caroline
said. And then, softly, "Well, who is de man, ef
you knows so—"

"Don't keep cuttin' me off!" Nan snapped. " 'Side
o' dat, her an' Willie—dis same Li'l Willie whut
stays right here on this place!—her an' him—"

The bed creaked, and Caroline said, "Sh-h-h—
hush," and stood up. She crept back to the bed and
Nan's eyes flashed red against the fire as she got to
her feet.

The girl's eyes were wide open now, regarding
Caroline weakly from the pillow. They were deeply
set and dark in their sockets, and her face looked
gray and worn, older. She didn't move or say anything.

"You feels lak eatin' a li'l bite now, honey?" Caroline said. "I done fetch some victuals here fer you."

The girl shook her head and wet her lips. Her lips were dry and parched. She said, "I jes wants some water."

"Well, I'll git you some water," Caroline said, and went back to the table where the bucket was. "Willie done jes fetched some from de well a while ago."

Caroline carried the dipper over to the bed, and Nan came and stood there by the foot of the bed, looking down at the girl.

"Dis water is cool an' fresh," Caroline said, and held the dipper close to the girl's mouth.

Ollie didn't try to sit up. She raised her head from the pillow and took a sip and swallowed; then sipped and swallowed again. She drank all that was in the dipper, and Caroline said, "You want some mo'?" But the girl only shook her head and dropped back on the pillow.

"Dat gal is got fever," Nan said.

Caroline looked up at Nan sharply and laid her hand against the girl's forehead. Then she went back to the bucket and wet a cloth. She placed the

238

cloth on Ollie's head and told Nan to get a dry towel to keep the pillow from getting wet. Nan got a towel from a nail over the table and brought it back to the bed, and Caroline placed it against Ollie's face next to the pillow.

Shadows were getting thicker in the cabin now. The sun had set. And the two women stood there by the bed, looking down at the girl. Her eyes seemed to grow brighter as the shadows thickened. They peered up out of their sockets, like tiny, peeping lights that burned far back in her head. Caroline and Nan remained silent, watching her eyes.

The girl moved her head a bit to one side, and the whites of her eyes slid out from under her lids. Her head became still again and her lips moved. She said, "Jule."

Caroline took a step closer to the bed and listened. The girl spoke again, and Caroline said, "Who you callin', honey? Who is—"

"I callin' Jule," the girl said, and Nan's face lit up.

"Dat must be de man dat gal done cut her 'bout," Nan said.

"Will you please hush?" Caroline said to Nan.

Then she turned to the girl and pressed the cloth gently against her forehead. She said, "Who is Jule, honey?"

"Jes Jule," the girl said. "He—he—"

She broke off and her eyes dropped back into focus —seemed to burn. She shifted her head on the pillow again, and said, "I want some mo' water."

Caroline went back to the bucket and got the dipper, and Alex came up the steps and entered the room, just as she lowered the dipper to the girl's lips.

The girl sipped once and swallowed. Then she shook her head and lay back on the pillow and closed her eyes.

Alex looked at Caroline and then at the girl lying there with the damp cloth about her head.

Caroline said, "She got fever, Alex. She done drunk water twice since she woke up, an' she been talkin' outa her head."

"How long she been woke?" Alex said.

"She jes woke up a li'l while ago," Caroline said.

"She done had anything to eat?"

"She sey she don't want nuthin' to eat. I done

fetched her victuals down here an' was keepin' hit warm by de fire."

"She ain't got no business eatin' wid dat fever," Nan said, "less'n hit was some soup or sump'n."

Alex looked at Nan and then at the girl. He said, "Guess you is right, Nan, for once."

"I knows I is right!" Nan said. "I been right from de very fust. Ef you all done listen to me, dat gal wouldn't—"

"All right, Nan," Caroline said. "I'll go fix her some soup, but hit ain't no need to go takin' on 'bout all dat now."

"Hit ain't a matter of takin' on!" Nan said. "I done told Alex from de beginnin' dat—"

"All right, all right," Alex said. "I ain't ask you whut you done told me!" He continued to look at the girl's face. The lids over her eyes were kind of wet-looking, and the rest of her face was a little white—dead white. He picked up her wrist and felt her pulse, and Caroline walked back to the table and placed the dipper bottom upwards over the bucket.

Then she turned and came back to the foot of the

241

bed. "I go fix de soup, Nan, ef you stay here tell I git back. Mae Jane is comin' back to set wid Ollie later on."

Nan looked at Caroline, her breathing sinking deeper into her bosom, but she didn't say anything.

Then Alex said, "Go on, I'll be round here a while."

Caroline picked up the cup and plate from the hearth and went out the door, and Alex dropped the girl's hand and lifted the cloth from her head and placed the other side against her flesh.

Nan turned and walked back to the fireplace and dropped down in a chair and stared at the fire.

CHAPTER XVIII

The doctor returned the next day, which was Sunday, and the day following, which was Monday. It was October. Nights were getting long and cool. The first frost fell the latter part of that week, and a cold stinging rain set in. The road through Hannon and Gerrington got sloppy and thick with mud, and travel, except on horseback, became slow and difficult.

Alex didn't send for the doctor any more that week. The rain continued. The three women—Caroline, Nan, and Mae Jane—took turns sitting with Ollie, and Slaughter and Willie kept firewood in the box and fresh water in the bucket. Alex came by twice a day and once during the night to look at the girl. Her pulse was erratic and her temperature mounted steadily. Alex said, "Soon as the rain let up, guess we'll have to see about gettin' her to the doctor." But the rain didn't let up, and the doctor's

243

fee was too high to come ten miles through the mud in the rain.

So the three women sat with Ollie, and each night Knute Kelly and Bell would stop by on their way from the field to ask how she was feeling. Occasionally, Uncle Len or old Hamp or some of the others from the Stand would pause in passing. And that Thursday Lucy West came over from Phillpotts' place and brought a bowl of chicken soup for Ollie.

"I done heard 'bout you bein' sort o' poorly," Lucy said, stepping up into the cabin out of the rain, "an' I done aimed to git by here befo'e dis. But us corn was yonder in de field an' hit done sot into rainin' lak hit is."

She placed the bowl on a chair beside the bed, and Ollie said, "Thank you jes de same, Mis' Lucy," and stared up at the older woman's face. Her voice sounded weak and thin, scarcely more than a whisper.

"Do you feels any pains, honey?" Lucy said. "I means—dat cut don't hurt you none, do hit?" She was looking directly at Ollie's face.

"No'm, I don't feels no pains," Ollie said. "I don't feels nuthin'. I jes feels like I is—is dead." She shifted her head on the pillow and stared up at the rafters and the wet, leaky roof, with the sound of the rain upon it. Then she turned and looked at Lucy's face again. "You know, Mis' Lucy," she went on, and her eyes were strangely vivid now—"You know, hit jes feels like somethin' inside of me been dyin' a long time an' all of hit is 'bout dead now, 'cept dat part dat ain't got no feelings."

"Honey, ain't nuthin' inside o' you dead," Lucy said. "Dat's jes yo' 'magination! You feels dat way 'cause you is weak fum loosin' all dat blood. You is jes dried out inside—dat's all."

"But dat's de way I feels," Ollie said. " 'Tain't like as if I was cold dead, like Della an' all de other peoples whut's done been buried in dey graves. Hit's jes like as if I done died all I kin die, an' dat part of me whut ain't dead ain't got no feelings fer dat part of me whut is."

Caroline brought a spoon back to the bed then, and said, "Here, honey, you eat some o' dis soup Lucy done fetch you. Den you gwine feel bettah." Then she turned to Lucy, and added: "De doctor sey she can't talk long at a time, Lucy. You know talkin' makes her feel sort o' weak-lak."

Lucy stood there an instant, watching the girl's face, then went forward to the fireplace where Nan and Mae Jane were sitting. She took a seat on the wood-box, and when Caroline returned to her chair, she said, "How come you all don't do somethin' fer de gal, Ca'line? No use to set here an' let her suffer lak dat! Fust thing you know she gwine be gittin' pizen in dat cut."

"De doctor been tendin' her," Caroline said, "an' Alex won't let us do nuthin' but what de doctor sey. An' de doctor sey jes to keep her quiet an' feed her victuals dat'll make mo' blood."

"You can't jes set here an' do whut dese fool doctors say," Lucy said. "Dey don't always know whut dey is talkin' 'bout. Y'all got to fix a po'l'ice an' put hit to dat place an' draw all de pizen outa her, an' ef y'all keep messin' around hit's gwine be too late."

"But Alex done sey to do whut de doctor sey," Caroline said.

"All right," Lucy said. "Go on an' do whut de

246

doctor sey, an' de fust thing you know dat whole left side o' her gwine to be pa'lized, too."

"She mought be bettah off pa'lized at dat," Nan said, and skeeted a thin stream of tobacco juice deftly into the fire.

Lucy turned and looked at Nan. She said, "Whut dat you sey, Nan?" But Nan only said, "You heard me!" and continued to look at the fire.

Caroline said, "Don't pay Nan no mind, Lucy. She jes talkin' to hear herse'f talk. Alex done told her 'bout talkin' so much when she don't know whut she is talkin' 'bout."

"Yeh; dat's whut Alex sey!" Nan said. But she didn't say any more.

Mae Jane hadn't said anything, and the others were silent now, watching the fire. The rain fell steadily upon the roof and the spoon made nervous, clinking sounds against the edge of the bowl, when Ollie dipped it into the soup.

The blaze died down and Caroline reached over and dropped another piece of kindling on the coals. Mae Jane sighed. Nan gnawed on the reed of her pipe, her elbows propped against her thighs, and old

Lucy sat stiffly in her seat there on the wood-box. Caroline sat up suddenly straight and the fire blazed again.

Then Lucy cleared her throat, and said, "Is she done told you all who done de cuttin'?" She whispered it.

"Nuh; she ain't sed nuthin' 'bout dat," Caroline said. "Alex done sey he gwine send fer de sheriff soon as de rain let up."

"Is Alex done ast her who done hit?"

"Yeh, Alex done talked to her 'bout hit," Caroline said. "But she nevah sed nuthin'."

"She ain't eben sed whut started hit or nuthin'?"

"Nuh, she ain't sed," Caroline said.

"Well, whut do she sey?" Lucy persisted.

"She don't sey nuthin'," Caroline said, and bent over to pick up her pipe from the hearth.

"She got a right not to sey nuthin'," Nan said then. "Hit's sump'n she wants to hide."

Caroline sat up with the pipe in her hand, but she didn't say anything. Lucy turned her head and looked at the fire again.

Mae Jane stretched and got to her feet then.

"Guess I'll be goin'," she said. "You gwine stay here wid her to-night, ain't you, Mis' Ca'line?"

"Yeh, I gwine be here," Caroline said. "Alex's comin' down soon as he git through tendin' de mules an' things at de lot yonder."

Mae Jane stood there wrapping a shawl around her shoulders and tucking the ends under her arms. Then she picked up an old coat and hung it over her head, and said, "Well, good night, you all," and went out through the door. . . .

Ollie was sitting up a little at the end of the second week, but she couldn't get out of the bed without assistance. Her side was still in stitches, and her face looked drawn and hollow about the eyes. The rain had continued without ceasing. But now it had dwindled to a thin mist, the wind driving it through the trees and over the fields, like powdered particles of dust. The clouds were low and frisky, the color of dull slate. They billowed over the fields and the wind kept getting sharper and colder.

Alex had hitched up the buggy that Monday

morning and put up the rain curtains and drove it up in front of Ollie's door. Caroline and Mae Jane had dressed Ollie and wrapped two quilts about her, and Alex and Slaughter helped her in the buggy. A brick had been heated and wrapped in baggins and placed in the foot of the buggy to keep her feet warm, and Alex had brought his lantern along to be used if the brick wasn't sufficient.

Caroline tucked the quilts about Ollie's feet and shoulders and drew the oil cloth up over her lap. Then Alex climbed in and drove off. He had hitched two mules to the buggy instead of one, on account of the mud and the rain. The wind was blowing harder now, the thin rain whipping in under the buggy top and wetting Ollie's face. It settled in bright, gray specks against her flesh, as she sat there on the seat beside Alex, staring out over the mules' rumps at the wet dripping fields.

The buggy rolled through the gap and headed down the road, and the wheels made a queer grinding sound as they dug through the ruts. Ollie was silent. She kept watching the road and the barren fields that flanked it on both sides. She watched

250

them with a vague sort of wonder, her eyes cold and unseeing.

It was noon when Alex drove into Hurtsboro and stopped in front of a hardware store. He helped Ollie out of the buggy and up a flight of stairs to the doctor's office over the store. Then he came back down the stairs again and watered the mules and fed them in the foot of the buggy, and went across the street to MacLeod's Feed and Supply Store to get Caroline a supply of snuff and tobacco and a bag of cane sugar.

Old Mack MacLeod was seated in his office at the rear of the store when Alex walked in; and when Alex had finished with his purchases, he went back there to have a word with the old planter before returning to the doctor's office. For forty years Alex had known MacLeod (had been his overseer back in the nineties at Hannon), and he rarely ever came to the 'Boro without passing a word with the old planter.

"Howdy, Mr. Mack," Alex said, squeezing his way through a passage between stacks of cotton-seed meal and entering the office.

"Howdy, Alex." The old planter wheezed through his nose and stared up at Alex. He made a hacking sound in his throat and held out his hand, the swivel chair bouncing up to a sitting posture and lurching forward. "What brought you in to-day in all this goddamn wet, Alex?"

Alex grinned and took the old planter's hand. "Had to fetch one of my hands in to see th' doctor," he said. "Had a li'l cuttin' scrape out my way a few weeks ago."

"Too goddamn wet to be slopping around with a fool nigger, Alex." MacLeod made that hacking sound in his throat again and stood up, glancing about the office. He was tall and stooped at the shoulders, this old planter, with bright baby-blue eyes placed deep in their sockets. A white beard jutted out from the lower part of his face, like hair on a goat's chin, and his stomach caved in through the middle, as though its inner wall had been glued to his backbone. "Been saving a bottle around here some'ers, Alex," he announced shortly, "if I can find it."

He hobbled over to a corner and began searching

252

through some old boxes there, and Alex said, "Much oblige, Mr. Mack. Was kind o' hopin' you'd have a li'l somethin' around. Sho' is damp an' chilly out."

Alex smiled again and MacLeod came back to his desk with a quart bottle held tightly about the neck between his fingers. He said, "No use to thank me, Alex. Any goddamn time you come to town you know there's always a bottle waiting here for you."

He inserted a screw and pulled the cork and poured two drinks in a couple of glasses there on the desk. He handed Alex one and picked up the other and made that hacking sound in his throat again. Alex grinned. They emptied the glasses and gulped once, the planter clearing his throat with a flourish.

"Goddamn fine liquor, Alex."

"Yes, suh, Mr. Mack!" Alex said.

MacLeod poured two more drinks, then corked the bottle and handed it to Alex. "Now you save some of that so Caroline'll have a little toddy," he wheezed, lifting the glass and tilting it against his mouth. The liquid slid down his throat and he gulped. "I mean, don't go drink it all before you

253

get home!" he went on. "Goddamn it, Alex, you drink much liquor as I can, once you get started."

Alex chuckled, breathing heavily. "Won't drink it all, Mr. Mack. Just needed a li'l swallow to take off th' chill."

Alex took a step toward the door and MacLeod held out his hand again. "Take care of yourself now, Alex," he said, "and don't go slopping around like this again with a goddamn fool nigger." He made that hacking sound in his throat again, his breath wheezing through his nose. "God, you're getting old the same as me, Alex. Can't afford to take chances like that."

"All right, Mr. Mack," Alex said, and went back across the street and up the steps to the doctor's office, with the bundles under his arms.

The doctor had finished with Ollie when Alex entered. The girl was sitting in the waiting room, with the quilts across her lap, staring at the floor. Her eyes seemed larger and she didn't lift her head when Alex entered. She simply sat there and stared at the floor, her eyes getting bigger all the time. She didn't seem frightened or anything.

Merely it seemed as though her eyes were things she couldn't control, and they went on getting bigger and bigger, and all she could do was sit there and watch the floor. Whatever it was that was affecting her eyes didn't seem important to her in the least. Probably it was something she could control, but her eyes couldn't conceal.

Alex said, "Well, how's it now, Ollie? Feel pretty good?"

There was a moment's silence while the girl lifted her eyes from the floor and looked at Alex's face.

"I feels pretty good, I guess," she said. "But I guess hit don't matter so much 'bout de feelings now." She looked at the floor again and the quiver of a smile touched her lips.

Alex stood there looking down at her, but she didn't say any more. Then the doctor stuck his head through the door marked "private" and beckoned to Alex to come back there. So Alex placed his bundles behind a chair in a corner and went into the doctor's office. He stayed back there quite a while talking to the doctor. Ollie could hear the low mumble of their voices behind the panel, and

255

she sat there with the quilts across her lap, staring at the floor, as though the things they were saying didn't matter to her in the least. She just sat there and waited until Alex came back through the door. Then she heard Alex say, standing there in the doorway that led into the doctor's private office, "But you kin be sho' in another week or ten days?" And the doctor said, "Yes, I can be fairly certain then—probably when I come out to take out the stitches. Anyway, it is she who admits the possibility."

Alex turned then and picked up his bundles, and went over to the chair where Ollie was sitting. The girl hadn't moved. Only her eyes showed that she might've been listening. . . .

It was dark when Alex drove the buggy through the gap and stopped it in front of Ollie's cabin. Caroline, Nan and Mae Jane were waiting there in the cabin door, with the firelight behind them, and a mule was tethered to a corner of the cabin with the saddle still on her back. The saddle was wet.

Ollie was looking at the mule and the saddle,

256

when Caroline and Nan came down the steps and rushed out to the buggy.

"Dere is a man waitin' inside, Alex," Caroline said. "He done come here to see Ollie."

Caroline paused and looked at Ollie's face. Then she said in a different tone: "How you feels now, honey?"

"Hit's Jule!" the girl breathed, and looked suddenly at Caroline and Nan.

"Yeh, dat's whut he sey his name is," Caroline said. "He come dis mornin' right after you all left."

Alex slid down from his seat to the ground, and Ollie continued to sit there in the buggy, watching the mule. She stared straight at the wet saddle, with the stirrups looped over the horn, and Caroline was silent. Nan was silent, too, watching Ollie's face.

Mae Jane stepped down out of the door and came toward the buggy, and Alex turned to Caroline and said, "Who you say he is?"

"Jule," Caroline said. "Dat's whut he sey his name is."

"Did he say what he want?"

"Jes sey he want to see Ollie," Caroline said. "See her 'bout—'bout—"

"He know she sick?" Alex said.

"Yeh, I guess he do know hit," Caroline said. "He sey—"

"You tell him she went to see a doctor?"

"Yeh, us tell him dat, too," Caroline said. "But he sey he gwine wait. He sey he—"

"Well, what he say he want then?" Alex said.

"Dat's whut he want," Nan said suddenly. "Want to see how bad off she is. He know all 'bout de cuttin' an evahthing. He eben know de gal whut done hit."

"All right, all right," Alex said. "Now hush up— all you!"

He turned and caught hold of Ollie and helped her to the ground. But she continued to look at the mule. Her eyes seemed to go straight through the beast and beyond, and rest on something that fascinated them in the distant mists beyond the swamp.

"Jule's saddle done got wet ag'in," she said, and there was silence.

258

The three boys—Slaughter, Shell and Willie—came from the cabin and took charge of the buggy and drove it up to the yard. And Alex helped Ollie up the steps into the cabin, the three women following close on their heels.

Jule was sitting in front of the fireplace. He looked around as Alex and the girl entered the door and stood up, his body silhouetted against the brightness of the fire His face was bright and wet. He said, "Ollie—Ollie!" and looked at the strangeness of the girl's face and eyes.

Ollie halted in her tracks, and Jule fell silent. Alex stood there beside the girl, his hand under her arm, looking at Jule. Jule's face began to sweat. His eyes expanded a little in their sockets and grew larger. He wet his lips and took a step forward. "You—you feels all right now, Ollie?" he said.

The girl remained silent, her eyes drifting farther and farther away. Alex didn't speak. The three women had crowded through the door and were standing there behind Alex and the girl, their faces lean and vivid against the firelight. Nan's mouth stood open; Caroline and Mae Jane had folded their arms tightly across their bosoms, and a queer still-ness filled the room.

Jule came quickly forward then and touched the girl's hand. "Hit wa'n't real bad, was hit, Ollie?" he said. "Hit wa'n't—"

Something in the girl's face seemed suddenly to change, and her body began to tremble from her head to her feet. Alex tightened his grip under her arm, and Caroline stepped quickly forward and caught the girl under her other arm.

"She takin' a chill, Alex!" Caroline said. "She takin' a chill!"

Alex didn't move. The lids slid shut over the girl's eyes, and her body became strangely still again. Jule withdrew his hand. The girl opened her eyes and looked at Jule.

"Yo' saddle done got wet, Jule," she said softly. "Yo' saddle done got wet an' you got to go back to Roba yonder!"

"Roba? I ain't gwine back to Roba!" Jule said. "I gwine stay here wid you. I gwine stay here tell—tell—"

The girl's eyes widened, as if startled, and her

260

body began to wilt. She said, "You got to go back to Roba, Jule! . . . You got to go back, an'—an' yo' saddle done got wet."

Her body swayed suddenly. Jule cried, "Ollie, Ollie?" and caught at her with both hands. But Alex pushed Jule aside, and lifted the girl bodily in his arms and laid her on the bed.

"She done fainted, Alex!" Nan said. "Don't you see she done fainted? You got to fix a hot tea an' put towels to her head!"

"Hush up!" Alex said, "an' do somethin'! Don't stand there holloing like you is crazy."

The cabin became feverish with action then, with the women rushing about, setting water to boil in three-legged skillets, and fetching wet towels and strong-smelling camphor back to the bed. Alex loosened the clothes about the girl's throat and waist, and held the camphor under her nose for her to breathe. Only Jule stood there in the middle of the floor, his arms hanging limply at his sides, as though he were lost. The women rushed past Jule and around him, going to and fro from the fireplace to the bed, and Jule stood there with streams of water trickling down the sides of his face, staring at the girl, while Alex worked over her.

When the girl opened her eyes and began to breathe evenly again, Alex turned to Jule and told him to take his mule to the lot and feed her, and to wait at the house with the other boys until he came.

CHAPTER XIX

JULE was still at Alex's when the sheriff came. His mule stayed in Alex's lot and he slept in the vacant room next the one where the other three boys were quartered. He ate his meals in Caroline's kitchen and talked to Alex when the others weren't around. The words between the two were simple and direct, for the truth wasn't a thing that Jule sought to hide. He told what there was to tell concerning himself and Ollie, and the other girl at Roba. He related the incidents, step by step, that preceded the cutting in the churchyard, while Alex sat and listened. Alex made no comment on the things that Jule said. He merely listened, asking now and then a further question, assembling what facts he could to be presented to the sheriff when he came.

The sheriff drove out to Alex's place on a Saturday. The day was brisk and clear, the balmy November sun imparting a certain calm to the

263

sharpness of the breeze. The other hands were busy at the syrup mill, grinding sugar cane and making molasses. They had been busy all that week. During the day, their voices were loud and tense with laughter as they toiled and sang at the mill; and at night, the smell of stewing cane juice, and the red, blazing fire, formed a backdrop for their rich voices and loud, country talk.

Early that morning, Alex had hitched the buggy and had gone with Jule to Roba in search of the girl who had cut Ollie. They went directly to the row of cabins where Jule lived, but the girl wasn't there.

"She done gone," an old woman told them. "She packed her things an' took to de road two, t'ree days ago. She nevah sey where she gwine. She jes packed her things an' took to de road. I seen her early dat mornin', wid a bundle on her back, headin' fer de Crossroads."

So Alex and Jule drove to the Crossroads, and then to Fort Davis, and found the girl hiding there in the quarters among the railroad section hands.

The girl seemed frightened when she saw Alex and Jule. She regarded them with quick, shifting

264

eyes, and said very little. Alex didn't ask her any questions. He merely talked to her in a quiet sort of way, explaining what he thought was best for her to do.

"Might save you a lot of trouble," Alex told her, "if you go back wid us. Sheriff is comin' out, an' it might be easier on you if you was on hand to say whut you have to say."

"But I ain't got nuthin' to sey, mister!" the girl said, with a startled look on her face. "An' I don't aims to go to no jail! Hit wa'n't me dat was in de wrong. Hit was dat other 'oman! She was de one dat stuck her nose in my business lak—"

"Ain't th' point," Alex said calmly.

"But I done tol' you I don't wants to go to no jail!" Her voice rose hysterically. "I jes don't wants to go to no jail, mister! I ain't los' nuthin' in no jail, an' I ain't done nuthin' wrong. Dat other 'oman was de—"

"Hit ain't whut you done wrong," Alex said. "Sheriff kin figger that out. Point is, if th' sheriff got to go about lookin' fer you, hit might make hit harder. But if you is on hand when the sheriff

come, hit'll show you ain't got nothin' to hide—
an' that's where hit'll be easier fer you."

The girl fidgeted. She stood there looking at
Alex and Jule, sucking her breath in deeply. Jule
was silent, looking at the ground. Then he shifted
suddenly in his tracks, and said:

"Uncle Alex is tellin' you whut's right, Lena. He
jes tryin' to help you—make hit easy fer you!"

"But I don't wants to go!" the girl said, turning
to Jule. "I don't wants to see no sheriff, an' I don't
wants to see dat other 'oman, neither."

But, in the end, she did go. She rode back in the
buggy, sitting on the seat between Alex and
Jule....

It was mid-afternoon when the Sheriff arrived.
The girl was waiting back in the kitchen with Caroline, and Alex and Jule were sitting on the front
porch. The other hands were still busy at the mill.

Alex stepped off the porch and had a talk with
the Sheriff. Then he went back to the kitchen and
got the girl and went with the Sheriff and Jule to
Ollie's cabin.

Ollie was sitting by the fireplace, watching a blaze that had been kindled there. The door stood open, and she could see the four of them, as they came up the steps, single file, and entered the cabin.

The Sheriff stood before the fireplace in the middle of the floor. Jule slumped down on a pile of wood in the wood-box, and the other girl sat on the edge of a chair facing Ollie. But she didn't look at Ollie. She looked at the fire, at the floor, and at her hands lying limply in her lap. Alex remained standing by the Sheriff's side, looking down on the trio sitting there.

The Sheriff did most of the talking. He looked at Ollie, and said, "You know this girl?"

Ollie glanced at the girl's face, and looked quickly away. She said, "I ain't sho ef I knows her or not."

"Ever see her before?" the Sheriff said.

Ollie glanced fleetingly at the girl's face again, and the other girl looked straight at the fire, her lower lip clinched between her teeth.

Ollie shook her head. "Ef I is, I don't 'member hit." She spoke as though she were scarcely conscious of the things that she said.

267

The Sheriff glanced sideways at Alex.

Alex said, "Th' Sheriff wants th' truth, Ollie. He come to find out th' truth."

"Dat's whut I tryin' to tell him, fer as I know," Ollie said.

"You mean to say, you don't know her and you don't remember ever seeing her before?" the Sheriff said.

"No, sir, I don't 'member hit," was all that Ollie said.

There was a pause. The Sheriff continued to look at the side of Ollie's face, with the firelight on it. Then he glanced at Jule and the other girl sitting there, his eyes glinting sharply against the brightness of the blaze.

He turned back to Ollie, and said, "Is this the woman that cut you?"

Ollie was silent. The other girl looked up and around sharply, and her thin face seemed to tighten. Jule didn't move. Alex didn't move. Only this girl, sitting there on the edge of her chair, seemed taut and restless. She twisted from side to side in her seat, moistening her lips, and her face began to

268

sweat. Her eyes grew frightened and round. She opened her mouth and snapped her teeth together with a brittle sound.

Ollie said, "De 'oman whut cut me, I nevah see her befo' in my whole life. An' dat night, hit happened so quick I didn't hab time to know whut she look lak or whut hit was all about. So ef she de one, I don't know hit, an' I don't guess dat make so much dif'ence now, neither."

Jule had got to his feet then, and looked at Alex and the Sheriff, huge drops of sweat gleaming on his forehead.

"I guess I is de cause of all dis," he said simply. "I guess ef I had done whut was right, all dis wouldn't hab happened.... But Lena here done de cuttin' lak I tol' Uncle Alex. I guess Ollie jes didn't want to sey hit. I guess she jes—jes didn't want to make no mo' trouble on account of Uncle Alex."

He paused, breathing heavily, and Ollie said:

"Hit ain't dat I don't wants to make no mo' trouble or nuthin'. Hit jes dat hit don't matter ef she done hit, or ef she didn't. I is cut now. An' when you is cut, you is jes cut, an' dere ain't nuthin'

269

nobody kin do fer you but sew you up—an' de doctor done already done dat!"

The Sheriff turned to Alex with an astonished expression on his face, and the other girl looked suddenly relieved.

"You don't want th' Sheriff to lock her up—is that whut you mean?" Alex said to Ollie.

"I don't reckon dat would do me no good now," Ollie said, and her eyes continued to look at the fire. "Ef she de one whut cut me, I guess she done hit because she figger she was doin' whut was right. An' I guess ef I had been her, I'd hab cut her jes lak she cut me. Hit was me or her—an' hit jes happened to be me!"

The Sheriff shrugged his shoulders and looked at Alex again. The girl called Lena sat up suddenly straight, and looked directly at Ollie for the first time. She didn't say anything. Just looked at Ollie's face, her eyes glazed with a kind of wonder. Her hands and body began to tremble. Her throat and lips twitched. With a sharp little cry, as if from a stab of pain, she leaped to her feet and bolted through the cabin door....

270

The Sheriff and Alex went out through the door behind the girl, and Jule stood there before the fireplace, looking down at Ollie. He stood there a long time without speaking. Then he sighed suddenly, and said, "I guess dere ain't nuthin' mo' to sey now, Ollie."

"Nuh, I guess dere ain't, Jule," Ollie said. She didn't lift her eyes or turn her head to look at him.

"Well, I guess I be leavin' to-morrow or de nex' day," Jule said then, as though it were just a thought. But Ollie didn't say anything to that, and Jule continued to stand there.

"Was sort of figgerin' on askin' Uncle Alex to let me stay a while an' help around de mill an' wid de hog-killin' to sort of pay fer my keeps," he went on in the same listless tone. "Was jes figgerin' on stayin' a while. Figgered dere mought be somethin' I could do."

He paused, as though he expected Ollie to say something. But she didn't. And he stood there, awkward and quite still, with the silence thickening about him. Then he turned and walked across the

271

floor to the door—then wheeled suddenly and went back to the fireplace.

His face seemed suddenly strange and bewildered now. He stopped beside Ollie's chair, bent over a little, and looked directly at the side of her face.

"Couldn't—couldn't us start all ovah ag'in, Ollie?" he said suddenly. "Me an'—an' you?"

The girl sat there a moment, as though she hadn't heard. Then she said, "Nuh, Jule, I guess not." Her voice was low and oddly peaceful. "I guess us was wrong from de beginnin', an' jes goin' on bein' wrong ain't goin' to help none," she added.

"But ef—ef us start right dis time, us wouldn't be wrong," Jule said. "Us—us could git married!"

"Mebbe hit wa'n't dat dat made us wrong, Jule," she said simply. "Mebbe us could hab been married an' still be wrong, an' mebbe us could git married to-morrow an' be wrong right on. I guess hit was somethin' more'n dat. . . . Seem lak us was jes livin' because us wanted somethin'—jes because us craved somethin'—an' us jes went on livin' jes fer dat. Mebbe ef dere had been somethin' us could want

272

an' not hab—somethin' us could work fer an' still want—mebbe hit mought hab been dif'ent."

Ollie paused, and Jule stood there, as if frozen in his tracks. He straightened suddenly and looked around queerly.

"De doctor gwine be comin' out to-morrow," Ollie said then. "He comin' to take out de stitches an'—an' tell Uncle Alex fer sho ef I gwine hab a baby. I guess hit ain't easy havin' a baby, when you stop to figger on de way peoples gwine look at hit. But hit's gwine be easy fer me. Hit'll be somethin' to live an' work fer—somethin' to dream about whilst I is sweatin' wid de sun flat ag'in my back. When you kin work fer somethin', you kin love hit; an' when you love somethin', you kin be happy widout tryin' to 'splain hit to yo'self. Lak eatin' yo' victuals when you ain't hongry. You kin eat hit, or you kin leave hit alone—but you is full right on!"

Ollie didn't say any more after that, and Jule was speechless. He simply turned and walked from the room, like a man in a dream....

After Jule had gone, Ollie continued to sit there a while, looking at the fire. Then she got up and went to the door, and gazed out into the cool Autumn dusk. She could hear the hands, laughing and singing at the mill, while they ground sugar cane and stewed the juice to a thick, scalding syrup. Their voices came loud and strong with the drift of the wind, and went rushing over the fields and through the swamp, like winged music echoing through eternity. The singing kept getting louder. It seemed to breathe and pulse with life, burning when it was sweet, and laughing when it was sad. It was life—a kind of living! It went on building itself, pyramiding itself, praying and hoping and laughing and sweating. And Ollie stood there and listened, while the dusk settled thickly among the trees and crept out over the still, twilit fields.

The dusk deepened. The singing became low and sweet. The sky turned black, and sparks from the chimney at the mill flecked it and went rushing onward and upward, spinning wildly, like jeweled spirits caught in the cross-current of the breeze.

Ollie stepped out of her door and walked across the field a little way, and paused behind a clump of bushes and leaned against the rail fence. She could

274

see the hands now, as they toiled and sang, their faces bright against the red glare of the fire. Slaughter, Shell and Willie; Nan and Mae Jane; Knute Kelly and Bell; Pink and her crowd, and all the others. Caroline and Alex were there, too, and old Lucy had come over from Phillpotts' place and had brought some of her gang. But she didn't see Jule.

Willie was feeding the mill, pressing huge stalks of sugar cane between the cylinders, while a mule pulled the long pole around and around. The others were busy around the vat, skimming the juice and dipping it up in huge ladles, and letting it fall, thick and hot, back into the vat. And all the while they sang. To-morrow, the doctor was coming out, and a week or two later it would be getting colder. Then it'd be hog-killing time, and they all would be busy cleaning chitterlings and drying up lard, and eating crackling bread. January would come and go, and February would slide swiftly in; and it would be time to start breaking ground again.

Alex had promised to give her a piece of ground to work for herself next year. He told her that on the way back from the doctor's office. "You kin have th' ten acres 'round yo' cabin," Alex had said. "Thank you, Uncle Alex," Ollie had said. "I kin work some fer you to pay fer de rent on de land an' a mule to plow hit wid." And that had made her feel happy in a way she had never felt before. She had something to look forward to—a farm of her own. And green things would live and grow that had been nurtured by the strength of her hands alone. Things that gave fruit in return for the sweat of her toil! ...

The air turned cooler, but the hands went on singing. Ollie turned and went slowly back across the field to her cabin. Walking again, her body felt free and light and strangely at peace, and something within her soul seemed to sing to the rhythm that floated out from the mill.